TAKE DAILY AS NEEDED

TAKE
DAILY
AS
NEEDED

A NOVEL IN STORIES

||||||||||||||||||||||||||||||

KATHRYN TRUEBLOOD

University of New Mexico Press | Albuquerque

Library of Congress Cataloging-in-Publication Data
Names: Trueblood, Kathryn R., 1960– author.
Title: Take daily as needed: a novel in stories / Kathryn Trueblood.
Description: Albuquerque: University of New Mexico Press, 2019. | Iden-
tifiers: LCCN 2019010527 (print) | LCCN 2019013523 (e-book) | ISBN
9780826360977 (e-book) | ISBN 9780826360960 (pbk.: alk. paper)
Classification: LCC PS3570.R767 (e-book) | LCC PS3570.R767 T35 2019 (print) |
DDC 813/.54—dc23
LC record available at https://lccn.loc.gov/2019010527

Cover illustration by Felicia Cedillos
Auhtor photo by Suzanne Blair
Designed by Felicia Cedillos
Composed in Sabon Lt Std 10/14

Some of the stories in this collection were previously published as noted below,
sometimes in slightly different form:

The Bellevue Literary Review: "The Medicated Marriage" (published as
"Unchecked") and "The No-Tell Hotel"
Blood and Thunder: Musings on the Art of Medicine: "Time Bomb Baby"
Conversations Across Borders: "Take Daily as Needed"
(published as "Patch Kit")
Literary Medical Messenger: "Taking My Father Hostage"
Los Angeles Review: "Fuck You! Till Next Christmas"
Referential Literary Magazine: "Anything but That"

Additionally, "The Whore of Healing" first appeared as
Diary of a Slut: Stories, an e-book published by SheBooks in 2014.

FOR GUNDARS STRADS,
MY TRUE BELIEVER

Contents

TIME BOMB BABY

| | | | | | | | | | | | | | | | | | | | | | | | | | | | | | | | | |

The first time our daughter, Noelle, was whisked off in an ambulance, she was fourteen months old. It was because I fed her pesto. Within minutes her lips distended. They looked like the slightly bent hot dogs that come in baby food jars. Our son, Norman, had never had a food allergy in his life, so I hadn't stopped for a second to consider that pesto contained pine nuts. I'd made the dinner because it was pasta. Kids like pasta.

Noelle's cheeks bunched up around her nose. Her whole face was surging like rapidly rising dough.

"What's happening to her?"

My husband, Guy, lifted Noelle out of the high chair. "She's having a reaction," he shouted. "Call 911."

I jumped for the phone and watched as Guy wet a washcloth one-handed. He held Noelle with the other, then pressed the cold cloth to her face. While I gave our address to the 911 operator, I fixated on my baby's face, on the dough rising, as though it were my job to watch until Noelle's features were expunged.

"Mommy," Norman yelled. "She can't open her eyes!"

After two days of administering prednisone, we could see Noelle's eyes again, two slits like scores in a loaf of bread. The allergist said reactive tendencies run in families. My mother was deathly allergic to eucalyptus, my grandmother to shellfish. "The tendency toward extreme reaction is inherited, though you can never know what the allergen will be. You can't predict severe reactions."

Afterward, Noelle was too terrified to be alone at night. I unfurled a camping pad on her floor. Every time Noelle startled awake, I said, "I'm here, sweetheart. Go back to sleep." Then Noelle would nestle back down on the crib mattress, and for a while I would drift along the crests of sleep, swaying like a cork at sea.

The second time we rode in the ambulance, Noelle was two and a half. Her Easter bunny did it, even though the ingredients list did not include nuts. We had read it very carefully. Later we learned that chocolate is the food at highest risk for contamination. Later the labels would all say "made in a facility that processes nuts" or "made on equipment that processes nuts." As I stood in supermarkets hyperventilating, they all read the same to me: "Will make you nuts."

In the ambulance I faced the back door, the asphalt ribbon of the road spooling out behind me—houses and lampposts attached like game-board squares. I held onto Noelle and kissed the top of her head. The medic was all the time talking, telling me what he was going to do. An epinephrine booster. He pressed the needle into Noelle's thigh, and she squawked.

"This should reverse the reaction," he said, after relaying Noelle's vitals into a black box above his pocket. Randy, the medic. My God he was handsome, in an action figure sort of way. I didn't catch the driver's name, maybe Sandy. Could it be true? Sandy and Randy?

"I am so relieved," I told Randy.

"We're going to monitor her heart rate," he said. "Epinephrine is really just a big boost of adrenalin."

I didn't expect him to look at me with the face of pure love. His eyes were bright with altar candles. But I wished he would put the IV needle away. The ambulance was jolting and jouncing like a goat cart. I couldn't believe Randy was going to stab Noelle's fat little arm. He did. Two jabs before I shielded Noelle's arms with my own. "Is this necessary?" I shouted into the din.

"We're almost there," Randy said, "we can wait," and he stroked Noelle's arm where the bruises would come. I gazed again out the back door. It was covered in schmutz. The coating muted the colors outside. I thought, *Someone really should clean that window.* Then I could relax on the ride, knowing that Randy and Sandy were in charge.

The third time Noelle was whisked off in an ambulance was because her preschool accidently fed her bread with ground pecans in it. A new employee had bought the bread from the local bakery. Five paramedics had stormed the little yellow house, marched right past the rice tub and the bubble maker and the lopsided easels. By the time I arrived the preschool director had administered the EpiPen, and the medics were monitoring Noelle's vital signs. They had isolated her in the foyer. I will always see it as a tableau—the lead teacher kneeling, the medic kneeling, and Noelle in her child-sized chair, arms drawn in, the hives on her cheeks rising in pink swatches, the silence she kept fixed like a seal upon her face.

Noelle is four and a half, and tonight at bath time she says, "My tushy hurts." Sometimes Noelle's skin is stung pink from uric acid if she hasn't been wiping. That's not the case this time. Clever girl, she just wants another stroke of the washrag; she knows what feels good. I can still see the purple marks on her arm where the IV line went in, the greenish bruise on her thigh where I pushed the EpiPen down hard. My heart thumps like a rabbit's back legs pushing off my chest wall.

"I think it needs more, Mama."

"Okay, sweetie, one more."

At night Noelle is in love with the story of our unity: mother and daughter. She wants to be the one to tell the story. "When I was in your tummy, I did whatever you did. I ate whatever you ate, and I sat when you sat."

"That's right," I say. "And I rocked you to sleep when I went walking." Noelle accepts this difference, since she knows that babies aren't born able to walk.

When I put Norman to bed, he, too, wants pillow talk. His teacher has been reading *Number the Stars* to the class. Norman peppers me with questions. "Did you ever know anyone who was in the Holocaust? Has anything that bad happened since?"

I avoid the gas chamber discussion, but I am careful not to duck his questions because Norman's mind does not diverge and recalibrate. I talk about history but attenuate facts: Srebrenica, the International Criminal Tribunal and the crimes of Milosec, the crimes of the Serbs against the Bosnians. I don't tell him about the images it conjures: boys in the backs of trucks, boys who become bones in the dirt, the grimaces of skeletons.

"What did he do to them, Mama? I want to know. You have to tell me."

I stare at the sparkles in the ceiling, knowing he will pester me for days.

"The soldiers marched people into the woods and made them dig trenches."

"What would happen if you didn't do it?" Norman asks, his whisper coming in warm, minty puffs against my face.

"They would shoot you."

"I wouldn't do it," he says firmly. "They'd have to shoot me."

I don't tell him they would have shot him anyway, in the back, so he'd fall face forward into his own grave.

"Yes," I say, "sometimes the only choice you have left is how you will die."

I thank Viktor Frankl silently for having safeguarded me in this moment.

"But it's still a choice," he says.

"Yes, now roll over so I can rub your back."

"I can't stop thinking about it."

"So let's say a list of all the good things this day brought."

When I come out of the children's rooms, Guy is in the living room watching TV. We alternate nights for putting the kids to bed. It turns out he is rigid about the parenting schedule, which is technically fifty-fifty, though I stay up much later, splitting my day around the kids. I work two part-time jobs—as a legal researcher and as a state-ordered mediator in divorce cases—and I type up the parenting plans and answer email from nine to midnight. I started out as a receptionist for a family-services office and ended up writing new documents to cover child-welfare program rules when state laws had to be brought into compliance with federal acts. It turned out I was good at it, and my shiny English degree was redeemed in everyone's eyes. The mediation I liked, especially the training in nonviolent communication. Since my father and mother each married four times, I've had some experience with listening to both sides in a divorce. My father always liked to say, "When both sides feel like they're getting screwed, you're close to done." He also liked to quote Zsa Zsa Gabor's famous line: "I am a maar-velous housekeeper. Every time I leave a man, I keep his house." Oh, how he loved to do her accent. "Dahling."

I have accepted Guy's and my schedule as the absolute equality of modern marriage: He gets up at 6:00 a.m., and I go to bed at midnight. After the kids are in bed, he relaxes while I go back to work. Since I am the one with the flexible schedule, as Guy often reminds me, I take on all the little extras, which lately don't feel so little or extra. Guy is not a bad man, he's just better at self-preservation. I'm starting to understand why he is dismissive about the details of the household—he doesn't remember them because he never had to, and though he talks a good line about equality in marriage, he is nonplussed about birthdays, Christmas shopping, teacher conferences, appointments with doctors and trauma counselors. He is the product of a stay-at-home mom, a scratch-and-sniff sexist; it's just a little beneath the surface.

Guy also has a way of winning the sleep lottery in our household. He falls asleep deep and fast—three quick breaths—and he stays that way unless I shake him by the shoulder to tell him Noelle is calling. Guy wins by lying passively in bed and waiting it out until I wonder, *What does it matter?* and get up myself. He also wins by being a grouch and yelling in the middle of the night. "Don't you dare get out of that bed."

Once I heard Noelle loudly proclaim to him, "You've made all my love go away."

After the third ambulance ride, which was eight days ago, I rented *The Secret Garden* for us to watch as a family, remembering the beauty of the garden sanctuary and the tale of childhood friendship. I had no memory of the scene in which Colin in his wheelchair is advanced upon by doctors wearing medical masks. Noelle screamed and fled the room. She screamed all the way down the hall to our bedroom. She slipped under our bed and wouldn't come out.

I lay on the floor and reached a hand toward our daughter. My reach fell just short.

"Noelle, Noelle," I called. "The little boy is going to be okay."

"No he's not," screamed Noelle. "He's going to *die*."

"No, he's going to get better and hike in the Alps with his new friend." I was confusing the story with *Heidi*, with *The Sound of Music*. What did it matter? Noelle was screaming so loud I don't think she could hear anything.

Guy's face appeared on the other side of the bed, vertical and flattened on one side just like hers.

"Ellie," he said, "it's just a movie. They're actors. It didn't really happen."

There followed a pause in Noelle's screaming. "It didn't really happen?"

"No, pumpkin. The boy in the wheelchair isn't really sick. He can walk."

"But the doctors were coming to get him."

"They're fake doctors, pumpkin. All fake. Come here."

I watched as Noelle scooched into his arms by pumping her butt up and down like a sideways swimmer. I was so grateful to my husband for knowing what to say; I had no words myself.

From my office window I see tundra swans hunkered down in the muddy fields. Winter is still with us, so many gradations of gray—drizzle, rain, condensation, slush. I fall asleep at my desk. I will never admit it, but I was glad to hand Noelle over to Danette today at noon. Danette is the youth minister of our church who watches Noelle while I work at the Dispute Resolution Center.

"Oh, pobrecita," said Danette in a cooing voice, "pobrecita bebé."
Yes, I thought: my darling, dearest, ticking bomb. Now I am catching up on typing Proposed Parenting Plans, dozing off between phrases, jerking awake at the keyboard.

Schedule for Children Under School Age. Prior to enrollment in school, the child(ren) shall reside with the mother except for the following days and times when the child(ren) will reside with the other parent: From Tuesday, 5:00 p.m., & Thursday, 5:00 p.m., to Wednesday & Friday, respectively . . .

Alarming fantasies arrive like small seizures. I have to shake my head in order to snap back to my computer screen. Each time, I can feel my head bending like a heavy bloom on a flimsy stalk. In my daydream the sheriff is calling to tell me that Guy has been in a terrible accident. I see myself wearing a black hat with a filmy veil, iconic, Jackie O's hat. Through it all I am a wonderful mother. I am noble in the face of loss. I never scream or burst into tears. After the funeral I take a nap while other people make dinner.

The droop of my head again reaches the snap-back point, and I push away from the desk in my rolling chair. I open the window and smell something flinty in the fall air, like pencil shavings. Lately, when I ask Guy how his day was, he answers, "Long," then stomps down the hall. In the kitchen he opens and shuts the drawers, looking for scissors or tape.

"What the hell. Why can't I ever find anything in this house?"

"Why should I know where the scissors are?" I ask.

I call it Irritable Male Syndrome, something that seems to have built up over time. Maybe Guy has a low tolerance for commotion; maybe he's fresh out of family time. My father-in-law takes his pipe out to a lawn chair and puffs away beneath his bird feeders while the rest of his family bustles and gabs indoors. Lately I wonder if Guy likes the idea of marriage more than he actually likes me. As myself, I am a constant affront to his sensibilities. I continually forget to do the wifelike thing. I don't believe in asking permission. I am impulsive. I let the children smash the ginger-bread house with hammers. I bring a dog home from the shelter without asking him first. I forget to draw the curtains before pulling off my clothes. I never want to leave a party when he does.

On the way home in the car, Noelle says, "Mama, poison apples look like any other apple."

"Yes, sweetheart, but it's the wicked stepmother who gives it to Snow White."

"I know, Mama, I know. But the witch looks like a nice old lady. She doesn't look like the wicked stepmother."

"But only for a few minutes, sweetheart. Then everybody knows."

"I'm scared of the apple, Mama. How can you tell when the apple has been poisoned?"

"Honey, poisoned apples only happen in fairy tales."

Noelle persists, "But the poison apple looks like any other apple." We're back to the beginning.

Yes, I think, and a piece of bread looks like any other piece of bread, except when it has ground pecans in it. I get a camping pad and sleep on the floor in her room. All night long, Noelle wakes, calling out, "Mama? Mama?" and all night long, I answer, "I'm here, sweetie. You're safe. Go back to sleep."

In bed at night I keep writing Proposed Parenting Plans in my head. Ones that aren't due until next week. *Schedule for Special Occasions. With Mother (Specify Year) Odd/Even/Every. With Father (Specify Year) Odd/Even/Every.* I take a deep breath the way I have been taught in yoga class and find myself gauging whether or not the Ambien is taking effect. I am not heavy-lidded yet. I miss the trazodone, which worked like an on/off switch, but I was never able to descend into deep sleep. Instead, I had the sensation of swimming through gelatin all night, a heavy, viscous substance that held me in place.

Next to me, Guy is snoring in short, loud bursts—"snorking," I call it. I sit up and dig in my top drawer for the foam earplugs I keep there, the fluorescent-orange kind that construction workers wear on site. My mind starts again in the cushy quiet. *Children's birthdays: May celebrate together if able. If not, each parent will have one child on his/her birthday during the year.* The huge photo on the front page of the morning paper competes for space in my brain—not the towers melting, not the falling man in the suit. It is the pair holding hands. Commemoration of 9/11. Guy left the paper in the place where his plate usually is. This morning, as I studied the handholding man and woman from my side of the table, they appeared to be drawn inexorably upward.

I make plans for the family to leave town for a weekend on the coast, thinking it will help us all to get away and start over. We drive north of Pacific Beach to a bare, blustery bit of Washington coast that backs up to the Quinault Indian Reservation. At night you look north into pure darkness until your eyes can't detect distance at all. When I close my eyes I can feel the darkness, smell the gusts of pine forest and brine. Sometimes a young brave or a disbelieving tourist will ignore the signs that warn against driving across the river at low tide. It's a pastime of the locals to watch cars sink into the Moclips River, even though everyone makes a good show of trying to pull them out with trucks and chains and winches.

At the beach Noelle is allowed to jump once from the jetty wall, like her brother who goes with her. That's what she does on Friday when we get here, but on Saturday morning Noelle takes off, straight toward the mighty breakers. She doesn't break stride when her pink plaid boots hit the water.

"Noelle," I yell. "Stop!"

Noelle looks back over her shoulder, then she goes right in to her waist.

"Noelle!" Guy yells. "Noelle!" But he is already running. I go on yelling, "Stop! Stop! Stop!" even after Guy has plucked Noelle from the waves, until I am saying it only to myself. I watch Guy bring Noelle back, holding her body against his chest with his forearms as though she were a rolling log.

When he sets Noelle on her feet, I go down on my knees, trying not to yell in her face. "Why did you run into the water?"

Noelle looks at me with ungenerous eyes, as though I ought to already know. "My body told me to. My body told me to run out into the waves and get sucked down and die."

It is the beginning of a dialogue, a dialogue between Noelle and her body. Each risk-taking event is a new test for us, her parents. Can we protect her when her body ups the ante?

We find a new preschool for Noelle, and I park in the preschool driveway and take notes on case precedents for my legal-research job. I do this every morning for three days. I can see Noelle's round head, her still-babyish face through the window, checking, checking, checking. I wave.

At the end of the day, I tell Noelle, "I stayed right there so you'd know you are in a safe place, so you'd know the adults are taking good care of you. But tomorrow Mama has to go back to her other job."

"I'm in a safe place," Noelle repeats in a trudging tone. "The adults will keep me safe."

The next day, an hour into a meeting with an attorney prepping for trial, my phone rings. At preschool, Noelle is hiding inside the puppet theater and won't come out. I step out into the glaring white hall of the new office building, which is sealed as tight as Tupperware, not a window that will open, and I listen to the bright, raucous sounds of the preschool, then the director's voice, "Come on, honey. Your mother is on the phone." Then I hear Noelle panting into the receiver.

"Mama, Angela threw up in the cubby room. Did the germs get on my lunch box? Will they make me barf? Will they give me the barfing flu? Mama? . . . I think I got nettle stings on my hand, Mama. They're bright pink. Am I having a reaction? Mama? Will it make me die? Will it make me barf? . . . But I can't, Mama. I can't stop thinking these thoughts . . . I got some bubbles in my mouth, Mama. From the bubble tub. Does that have bad chemicals in it? Mama?"

For two days Noelle won't eat at preschool: not snack, not lunch, not a bite. On the way home I weep. She wants to give away our dog because he coughed up some grass the night before.

"No, it was more than a little. Let's give him away, Mama. I don't care if Tater's our dog, Mama . . . I thought he would never stop. Can we give him away, Mama? Let's give him away . . . I won't miss him. Let's give him away . . . My stomach hurts, Mama, my stomach feels bad. It feels so bad I want to die . . . I know, Mama. My pillow is on the bad-dream side. Let's turn it over when we get home. Let's turn it over to the good-dream side."

Day three is the same. Noelle takes refuge beneath the puppet theater and won't come out.

"Mama, I got a splinter in my finger. It's under my skin . . . it got inside me. Mama, am I going to have a reaction? Mama? . . . A voice from God inside me tells me that if I go on the playground, I'm going to die, Mama . . . I know, everyone washes their hands, but not everyone sings 'Yankee Doodle' all the way, Mama. The children might have nut dust on their hands . . . Did Tater barf again? Mama? . . . I know, but he could do it again. How will we know? We should give him away, Mama."

"We should just bring Noelle home," Guy says after dinner. "You can quit the mediator thing, for summer at least."

"There's no guarantee they'll take me back," I say. "But I can't stand any more of this for Noelle either."

"It's a nonprofit, Maeve. The center doesn't pay you enough to justify the childcare bills."

"All right. What about our vacation?"

"We'll have to cancel our vacation plans. Our folks can fly out here if they want to see us this year." He leans back in his dinner chair with his arms behind his head. I admire his certainty. I need it. I haven't slept through the night in so long there's an intermittent buzz in my ears as though I were transmitting radio signals.

It is settled. I will work half-time this summer, and Noelle will spend it clinging to my knees. We only have to make it through my two-week notice. I call Danette to see if she can manage to do mornings as well as afternoons, but Danette is selling vacation time-shares online. She has a friend who might be interested in looking after Noelle. I decline. Noelle needs to be with someone she knows. Danette calls me back and says she can make it work if I bring Noelle over to her house, but it will cost more. I say we're just glad she can do it.

At 6:00 a.m., when Guy's alarm goes off, he shakes me. I have already been up with Noelle twice during the night. I pull out one earplug and look at his outline in the fuzzy light. "Noelle's up," he says, "and I've got to go."

"I can't," I say, my voice a creak. "It's your turn."

"I'll be late."

"Then be goddamn late," I shout, throwing the covers off my legs, fueled by a rage that makes me shake as though I were steam powered.

I march toward the kitchen, but I halt when I see the outline of Norman's tent outside. We left it set up after a weekend sleepover, and he likes to sleep in it even though the spring mornings are still crisp. I can hear Noelle's rising screams as I push the glass slider shut behind me.

Let him go to her, I think.

"Hey, Mom," Norman says, after I get the zipper door open. The air is grass sweet, and I skinny into the neighbor child's sleeping bag, which comes up to my chest.

"You sounded like the executioner in there," Norman says, turning onto his side. He has a voice from the Vienna Boy's Choir and a noble, seeker's face. He's been learning about how catapults work to lob mortars and flaming hay, spending his free hours painting tiny warriors in medieval armor.

"I bet I did," I say. "Oh, what the neighbors must hear on a daily basis."

"I sure wouldn't want to live next door to us."

"Me either, and it's a good thing you don't do any of the yelling." I make my voice drip with sarcasm, hoping to amuse him.

"No way," he says.

"Remember the time you dissected a hot chili pepper because you wanted to save the seeds for a practical joke?"

"Yeah."

"Afterward you forgot to wash your hands, but you picked your nose."

"No way."

"Yeah way—your nose actually bled. I think you yelled for an hour."

"Now I remember. Nothing stopped the burning."

"Sometimes there's no cure, unfortunately," I say, fingering the netting across my window.

"You should come out here more often, Mom."

"You're right. Maybe I should set up my own tent."

In the trauma counselor's office, Noelle plays with a boat on the floor. She rocks it through the waves. The trauma counselor is a long-limbed, tawny woman with glistening eyes and a heady laugh. I am skeptical because Dr. Gutierrez is young and doesn't have children of her own. The night before the appointment Guy said to me, "Some people have a really vivid memory of being a child."

The therapist lowers herself onto the floor with Noelle. Dr. Gutierrez speaks in a big, emphatic way that I am sure Noelle will find false, but Noelle seems to like her.

"Wow, looks like a storm," Dr. Gutierrez says.

"It is. A stormy storm."

"Who's the captain?"

"Nobody knows," says Noelle, her lips wet from the little bubbles she has been making.

"Huh, nobody knows. What does he do in the storm?"

"His boat gets a hole in it and he drowns."

"Bummer. He drowns. Is that the only ending?"

"Yes," says Noelle with finality, looking up to meet Dr. Gutierrez's lively brown eyes.

Dr. Gutierrez laughs, which startles me. "Not in my story!" she says. "In my story he takes the boat behind an island and hides from the wind. Or he sails up a river and waits for the storm to be over."

Noelle studies the doctor, whom she is allowed to call Wendy, though I have yet to hear Noelle use it. "What if he is blind?" Noelle asks, playing her trump card.

"Well," Dr. Gutierrez says jovially, "he'll ask his crew to help him."

Noelle squares her shoulders and stares, disconcerting in a four-year-old. I recognize the look. "He doesn't have a crew," she says with strained patience.

"Well, he better get one then!" says Dr. G, slapping her thigh and looking around like it's the most obvious thing in the world.

THE MEDICATED MARRIAGE

||||||||||||||||||||||||||||||||

"We can't know for certain the comorbidity of these diagnoses, though labiality is certainly present."

I scrutinize the lean, young psychiatrist whose attention is taut in the moment. He is a good ten years younger than I am, and he is speaking to me without a trace of paternalism. At least that's how I read him; he is honoring my intelligence by expecting me to know these words. When I cross my legs, I feel his eyes dart from the clipboard in his hands to my calves, which are glossy in sheer stockings. Most women my age have given up sheer stockings and heels. I notice he is wearing European man-clogs, which of course mark him as a progressive.

I try to return his serious stare, but I am thinking about the preponderance of facial hair among hip psychiatrists and history professors. He seems to take my look as a sign of comprehension. We have exactly five minutes because my son has already used up the first twenty-five, as per the agreement, and the session is only thirty minutes long. That's how the insurance company likes it—one hour for evaluation and diagnosis followed by half-hour med checks. My son Norman has been taking Ritalin for exactly two weeks. I can picture him, sitting outside the door in a purple chair, his brain pacified by the sixty frames per second of his Game Boy.

At the university library where I often do legal research, I find the Diagnostic Psychiatric Manual—or DSM-IV as it is known—and grudgingly admire these new words. "Comorbid" makes it sound as though the diseases that might kill you are cohabitating, which they are, as it turns out. I find nothing under "labiality," but I find "labile." That must be what he meant, and it has nothing to do with a woman's labia and everything to do with mood swings. But best of all is "emotional incontinence," which might well describe how I feel the week before Christmas.

Norman is nine and Noelle is five, but the holidays are especially hard on Norman. First of all, there's the Kris Kringle mystery gift exchange in his class.

"Mama," he says in the kitchen, "what if it goes to a girl instead of a boy?"

"It won't matter because it's a yoyo," I explain again.

"I know, but it's a red yoyo, and when you think red, you think boy."

This may be true—how else to explain red race cars and the Marlboro man? I watch him picking wax off the candles on the table. He has my dramatic features; the width of his jaw is the same as the length of his face. It's only when you meet stage actors up close that you realize their mouths and noses appear almost oversize, their eyes set deep.

"I had red rain boots when I was a girl," I say.

"Do you think the teacher will let us trade? I don't want a plate of brownies like last year." It's as though he hasn't even heard me.

"The point of a Kris Kringle," his father interjects, "is to focus on the act of giving rather than getting the present." I feel my husband's eyes on me and look up. The plates are on the table; the children are in their seats. Guy's eyes are the same soft amber as his hair. "Thank you for dinner," he says. Briefly, we clasp hands as husband and wife, and for a moment I think Guy will say the family grace he reserves for holidays—*Dear Lord, thank you for this gift of food you've placed upon our table. And help us all to do your work, in any way we're able. Through Christ Jesus, our Savior, Amen*—but instead he has to be quick to keep Noelle's cup from tumbling off the table.

Norman drops his head between his shoulders and lowers his mouth until it is even with the edge of his bowl, then he begins hoovering tortellini. His five-year-old sister, Noelle, is rocking her booster seat against the wooden chair.

"I did a wetlands inspection today," Guy offers.

"Oh?" I say, finishing a bite.

"Yeah, the developer was trying to convince me it was only seasonal drainage when this big, old beaver pops his head up."

"Do we get to hang ornaments tonight?" asks Noelle.

"Shh. Let your father finish."

"That's it. That's my beaver story."

Guy looks from one child to the other, then back to me.

I smile. "Hunting beaver at work again, honey?"

"Please, can we hang ornaments?" Noelle asks.

"Shut up," Norman says.

"Norman," I say, "she has every right to speak."

"She's stupid," says Norman.

His father sets his glass down hard. "No, she's little, and believe it or not, you were once five years old, and even more of a pain in the rear."

"Guy," I say, formally enunciating his name. Norman looks from one parent to the other.

"For the love of God, can't we ever just eat dinner?" Guy bellows.

"Norman is staring at me," says Noelle. "Make him stop."

"Apparently not," I say.

Norman gets up from the table without pushing his chair back. His thighs bump the table. The drinks slosh in their glasses. "I'm done," he says. "What's for dessert?"

"You've got to stop bolting your food," says his father, snatching a piece of pork off his fork with his teeth and bearing down hard on it.

"Did you have any salad?" I ask.

"Can we do the gingerbread house?" asks Noelle.

Norman stands in front of the refrigerator, fending off the door with one elbow while pouring milk into his glass. The door swings back, bumping his elbow, and milk sloshes to the floor.

"For Christ's sake," says his father, slamming his knife to the Formica.

"What?" shouts Norman. "What did I do wrong?" He stomps down the hall with his sloshing glass. His father looks toward the ceiling. I close my eyes.

Norman's stricken child face is burned upon my retina, and even though hours earlier I myself had yelled, "Goddamn it, Norman, close the back door," my heart produces a small pit and pushes it into my throat, so that before I can stop myself, I have said, "Guy, do you have to shout?"

"Unbelievable," says Guy, throwing his napkin onto his plate.

"I'm sorry," says Noelle, starting to cry.

"You didn't do it," I say, though who did is not apparent.

I help Noelle set cookies on a tray. They aren't homemade although they look that way. I have rolls of premade dough in the freezer, which I slice up whenever there's a school fundraiser or a soccer team match, but instead of putting the slices directly on the sheet, I roll it into balls between my palms and smash it with a fork. My husband comes into the kitchen and stands behind me— he has to because it's a narrow bowling-alley kitchen. He puts a hand gently on my shoulder. "Thanks for dinner, Maeve."

"Such as it was," I answer, smiling ruefully.

"Let's see if we can salvage the evening."

"It's pretty late," I say, "for a school night."

"Well, I'll tell the children we can hang ornaments until eight thirty."

"No," Norman yells, "that's not how we did it last year."

I busy myself with hanging Jiminy Cricket. I hand a fluffy lamb to Noelle, murmuring, "Here, honey."

"Do you even remember how we did it last year?" Guy stands stock still, a silver ball dangling in one hand.

Ooh, bad move, I think.

"Last year we hung them until nine o'clock and then turned the lights out." Norman has not fully entered the room. He is standing midway between the couch and the kitchen, yelling.

"This is what we did last year, too, honey. We hung a few ornaments each night, then on the last night we turned the living-room lights out. You just don't remember."

"No we didn't. That's not what we did."

"All I know," says his father, trying for a lighter tone, "is that we're done by eight thirty."

"Why are you ruining everything?" Norman yells at us, his parents. "Why are you trying to restrict everything?"

"You have a choice," says his father, and I complete the sentence with him, "either stop yelling or go to your room." We've been coached well by the family counselor (not to be confused with the psychiatrist).

Norman clomps down the hall, doing his best to make zombie footprints. Guy and I exchange weary looks over the tip of the Christmas tree. Noelle, meantime, is rummaging in the boxes of ornaments. "Look," she says. "I found the best angel."

I take the ornament in my hand—it has cleavage and big hair, all frizzy gold. I turn it toward Guy so he can see. "I call this one the Angel from Vegas." We dare to smile together.

"Don't you like her, Mama?" asks Noelle.

"Of course I do, Ellie. There's a place for every ornament on this tree."

We hear the door down the hall wrench open; it bounces against the doorstop. I think the very hinges of the house must hurt. I close my eyes and hear chorale music: "Dona Nobis Pacem," the simplest prayer, ancient as stone, "Grant Us Peace." When Norman appears, he takes up right where he left off. "Why can't we hang them like last year, until we're done? Like last year."

"Son, give it a rest," says his father. "This is how we're doing it."

Norman throws himself on the floor behind the couch. "This isn't how we're supposed to do it," he yells into the carpet.

I move a box of ornaments so that I can step around the couch and put a hand on his back.

"Don't touch me!" Norman shrieks. He jerks around in fury. There are creases beneath his eyes and drool on one cheek.

"Go to your room," shouts his father, swinging one foot wide over the boxes, ready to enforce it.

But I hold one hand out. An image of Guy dragging Norman by his heels, splay-legged down the hall, blots out the moment. Another image follows, this time Guy dragging Norman from under his armpits and the boy hooking his feet into the door jambs. We've been told not to move Norman now, not to escalate these emotional storms. I step back toward the tree in time to catch Noelle, who is tripping over the cookie tray. Norman is screaming: "No, I won't. I won't. I won't."

We go on hanging ornaments while Norman lies on the floor sobbing.

"I waaa-nt to dec-o-rate the Chris-t-mas tr-ee-ee."

"Too fricking much," says Guy, leaning down and scooping up Noelle. "Let's go have us a story."

I sit on my knees beside the tree. Our modest tract house is ten or twelve feet from the neighbors on either side, and I am grateful that neither of them has called CPS in the last year. Norman yells so loud and long, his speech is unintelligible. I think of the ancient mariners who strapped themselves to the mast so as not to be lost at sea in horrific storms. *Where are we all headed?* I wonder. *How shall this end?* Eventually, I will bring Norman a glass of water and offer it to him, and he will sit up and sip it tentatively, like a sleepwalker coming awake, later following me into the brightness of the bathroom and the soft darkness of his own room.

By eight thirty in the morning, I have already driven carpool, taking Noelle along in her dinosaur boots, which are on the wrong feet. These are the only shoes Noelle will wear and the only way she will wear them. Norman has holes in the backs of all his shirts where he has cut the tags out, and he has cut off the tops of all his socks as well, claiming they itch his ankles. A friend once said to me, "The problem is you have two 'only' children."

On Fridays I'm not due at the domestic law office of Slater, Steiny & Alesandro until noon. So I am alone at the kitchen table with a form from the psychiatrist in front of me—the NICHQ

Vanderbilt Assessment Scale: PARENT Informant. I've already looked up NICHQ—the National Initiative for Children's Healthcare Quality, which hasn't alleviated the guilt I feel over the word *Informant*.

The form lists symptoms in one column along with numerical designations, starting with 0 for Never, 1 for Occasionally, 2 for Often, and 3 for Very Often. Guy and I have already turned in the family tree of mental illness—Great Uncle Maynard, who received shock treatment and lived with his mother (after he served in World War II); Great Aunt Elsa, who took her phone calls in the closet and lived out of steamer trunks (don't the wealthy get away with whatever whey want?); my sister, who spent four years in the bathroom between breakdowns, studying what she believed was the matter with her face (okay, Mazie was definitely diagnosable, but she lives independently now, and they'd never caught Norman obsessing in the mirror); Guy's grandmother, who had taken her youngest daughter with her down to the Ohio River, then carefully folded her clothes and walked in (no question of depression there); and my mother, who had a nervous breakdown in the 1950s and was briefly institutionalized (didn't that happen to almost every white woman back then who wasn't doing well with Valium, cigarettes, and martinis?).

Then there was my father, a catastrophic thinker extraordinaire. He wouldn't let any of his grown sons light the barbeque for fear it would explode, and he did have the peculiar habit of rinsing paper plates before putting them in the trash. On the other hand, who wouldn't want an OCD surgeon? Someone who washed his hands repeatedly, checked and rechecked the sutures before closing his patients back up. My cousins, I wasn't sure about, though Uncle Galen definitely drank and smoked himself to death, and a few of the cousins had died in high-speed car crashes that made suicide anybody's guess.

The truth of it was we couldn't know. In my view, childhood itself is a kind of psychosis. Hadn't I read the same book thirteen times as a girl? And my brother had flushed M-80s down toilets and gotten kicked out of schools and punched holes in walls and driven any vehicle too fast. One morning he romped on the gas of the old Mercury station wagon while backing out of the driveway. A door flew open and tore off on a tree because he'd neglected to close it. Our mother was watching from the kitchen window. When did she have her nervous breakdown, before or after my brother was out of the house? But he'd turned out all right. He was a helicopter nurse, and you'd be lucky to meet him if that's where you ended up. Maybe Norman was one of those men who needed a high-risk profession to keep his attention, and a little manic energy was good when you had to power through an emergency.

I frown at the form and take up my pencil. I am frightened and I know it.

Does not pay attention to details / Has difficulty keeping attention to what needs to be done.

In first grade Norman fell in love. He was paying attention very closely. Everywhere the girl put her hands, he followed after, trying to put his in just the same place.

I check "Occasionally."

Does not follow through when given direction / Has difficulty organizing tasks and activities.

Every night Guy or I sit with him while he does his homework, otherwise he skips problems, pages, or whole chapters. He hates homework the way you hate someone who has betrayed you. From the time he was very small, insects and the beetle-covered undersides of logs captivated him. He studied the worms that came out onto the patio in the rain. While other children screamed at the larval world, he peered closer. His reflexes were so quick he could catch fish with his feet.

I check "Often" and glance down the page.

Loses things that are necessary for activities / Fidgets or squirms in seat.

Don't all children fidget? It's true that I find Norman's homework balled up in his laundry on the floor, sometimes assignments he has done already that don't get turned in. And when he had to learn his play lines, we came up with the novel idea of his using the elliptical trainer in the garage. He looked like a boy in a taffy pull, but he worked hard, shouting his lines as he pulled and pushed his arms and legs in opposing directions.

I check "Occasionally." I'm not going to pathologize intensity. Some people make it through life on Bunsen burners; my son is a bonfire. I've told him that in middle age when other people's energy wanes, he will have plenty. I let my eye bounce down the page.

Runs about or climbs too much when remaining in seat is expected / Talks too much.

Runs about? Talks too much? Had anyone who'd written this form read children's literature? It could have been a character-traits list for Pippi Longstocking. I wish I too could throw adults across the room. Tom Sawyer and Huck Finn were doomed also, according to this list. I myself had been like Fern, who talked to spiders and pigs all day and preferred their company to other children. After one week of first grade, Norman told me, "We just sit in a circle while that lady yammers all day." Norman is like Milo in *Phantom Tollbooth*, bored to tears by the adult world. When the music teacher asked Norman, "What farm animal are you?" Norman told her, "A cobra." When I made him choose again, he said, "A dust bunny." He doesn't play the part of the Disneyland kid for whom a sucker or an ice cream cone makes everything all better. I check "Often" because these points I can argue.

Actively defies or refuses to go along with adult requests or rules.

This is a definite. I would have checked "Every Single Day" instead of "Very Often" if that had been on the form. Norman doesn't respond to the politically correct forms of parenting. When he was four and five, I would have had to use bungee cords to keep him in a time-out chair. When I sent him to his room, he whipped out his willy and peed on the floor. Once I let him run straight into a lake fully clothed because I'd been chasing and tackling him for months. Was that in Dr. Spock's index? Each morning I lie still in bed for a few moments, praying, "God give me the stamina to get through this day."

Deliberately annoys people.

Did the time he kicked out all the floodlights in his grandparents' garden count? There wasn't anybody around. He wept when they made him empty his piggy bank. I rest my forehead on my palm. As a child I put dog doo in my aunt's shoe, just to hear the woman scream. My aunt couldn't see a thing without her glasses and slept in a bed full of yappy, snappy dachshunds. I had forgotten this story, buried it along with the memory of soaking a paper bag in gravy and Tabasco sauce and trying to feed it to the dachshunds. Maybe I was envious of the dogs, but I acted absolutely without analysis, as most children do.

Loses temper / Is touchy or easily annoyed by others.

Norman refused to come in from recess and was found beating the school building with his lunch box. He is not good at transitions. On parent night I counted eight different times the children had to put away or clean up in the course of a day. Not counting the twenty-minute lunch, which was fifteen minutes by the time they got their tray and their milk. And then there were the bells. Norman startled or winced when he heard the bells. By Friday all he wanted to do was stare into the pond-water tank. He could tell you the difference between bullfrog eggs and spring peepers.

When his teacher put her hands on Norman's shoulders to guide him, he threw up his arms and shrieked, "Don't touch me." She wanted Norman put in the after-school anger-management group.

Argues with adults.

"But what if the thing he is angry at is school?" I asked the principal during our meeting.

"Well," he said, "it's like vacuuming. I tell my kids that we'll get to the fun stuff when the vacuuming is over."

"Education is not like vacuuming," I said. A deep silence followed. Then he suggested I make a chart and use stars for Norman's good days. Or a system of poker chips for good behavior, rewarding with points and subtracting points. Maybe it worked for some families, but I couldn't see it working for ours. My life is complicated enough with having to learn case-management software and secure file sharing. And what point would Norman see in it? He'd rather be shot than bow his head for anyone, much less poker chips and stars. Yes, sometimes I wish he'd conform for thirty seconds, but I also love him for refusing the world as it is. Isn't that the role of visionaries and artists? I check the noncommittal "Occasionally" again.

Next I hit a set of "symptoms" I can easily breeze through.

Bullies, threatens, or intimidates others / Starts physical fights / Lies to get out of trouble.

I have the sensation of swooping down a slide as I briskly check a spate of "Nevers."

After school Norman barricades himself in the front hall closet and sobs. He won't come out. This is what the doctor described as the "Ritalin rebound effect." Norman usually isn't hungry at lunch, but by school's end he is desperate. When the stimulant wears off it dumps him emotionally, which I can generally forestall by giving him a snack the minute he gets in the car, but today I forgot. Now I can't get Norman to come out of the closet, and Guy is due home soon, and I need to take Noelle to the neighbor's so we can make the third appointment with the psychiatrist.

"Please, Norman, please. You'll feel better if you eat," I plead from outside the door.

"Leave me alone!" he yells.

I see Noelle around the corner, rocking in her booster seat. "Stop it, Noelle!" I shout, and then Noelle bursts into tears. I walk to the sink and splash water on my face. A child's plastic cup seems to be wedged in the garbage grinder, rim to rim.

"Hush, Noelle. I'm getting you some juice." I slam the refrigerator door, and plastic alphabet letters fall off. "Goddamn it," I yell, kicking them around on the kitchen floor and sideswiping a few under the fridge.

"My God," says Guy, coming into the kitchen. "I stood in the garage listening and held onto the doorknob. What is going on in here?"

By now I'm sniveling into my sleeve. I jerk my head toward the front hall. Norman can be heard through the closet door, sobbing and screaming: "I want ever-y-body to le-eeave me alone. Lee-ee-ave me alone."

"He hasn't had his snack, or his third dose," I say.

"When are the side effects supposed to wear off, that's what I'd like to know," Guy shouts above the fray.

Guy goes to the closet and stands with his feet planted hips-width apart. "Knock it off," he yells so forcefully that everything goes completely quiet. I pick Noelle up with a dishrag over my shoulder, lifting her out of her seat. Noelle wraps herself around me the way I remember baby chimps wrapped around Jane Goodall.

"Open the door, Norman."

"No! Go away!"

"I'm your father, and I'm not going away." Guy pulls at the door, which resists only briefly before a scrawny arm appears, then quickly retracts. Guy reaches in the closet, but I can't see what happens next. Bumping noises and scrabbling follow. Then Guy reaches in with both arms and lifts out our boy along with the vacuum cleaner he has clutched to his bosom.

"Okay, buddy," says Guy, kneeling. "Let's get you something to eat." Norman whimpers but doesn't resist as his father lifts him by one arm and leads him to the kitchen. "I've never seen anybody ride a vacuum before."

In the car on the way to the psychiatrist's at last, Guy lets out a big sigh through his nose. It makes a sound at the back of his throat like a low growl. Norman is in the back with his Game Boy, earphones on his head. I reach back and pat his knee. He looks up and gives me a small smile. Outside, the season shows itself. The alders, poplars, and maples are bare, the world a stark and scratchy place.

"I want him off the drugs," I say suddenly.

"I want to do what the science supports," says Guy.

I hate it when he uses that rigid tone. He sounds like the lawyers I work for who use the word "inappropriate" to discuss their colleagues' behavior. In some cultures drinking out of the skull of your enemy is appropriate.

"Don't give me that objective stance, Guy. It's a bunch of white male doctors."

"Have you studied the clinical trials?"

"No, but I have done some research. They used that shit in World War II. General Rommel doped the North African troops with amphetamines. The Allies gave the troops Ritalin."

"Maeve, this is no time for feminist history." He punches out a left-hand turn as the oncoming cars accelerate.

"What? Are you putting me in my place?"

"Don't twist my words."

"I don't have to, you said them." I roll down my window even though it is cold. It makes me feel as though I have walked out of the room and into another.

"Could you not be a bitch for once?"

"Nice, Guy. Really nice. No wonder he listens to you and not to me. He's picked up on your attitude."

"He listens to me because I'm firm and consistent."

"And what am I, then, some fucking noodle?" In my peripheral vision I register movement in the back seat and lower my voice. "I'm the one who goes without sleep while you're snoring away. Noelle wakes me up every freaking night crying."

"Yeah, and I'm just having a picnic doing the morning commute while you sleep in."

"I'd love a morning commute. It'd be a fucking meditation compared to getting these kids ready and driving car pool."

Guy swings hard into a parking place. "We're here. Are you done?"

"Yeah, I'm done," I say, my mind echoing with the incompletion—done with you, done with all of you, done with this nightmare called family. I don't know myself what I mean by it, but I feel a flicker of pleasure to see some fear in my husband's face.

We leave Norman in the purple chair and enter the psychiatrist's pointy office—it's a hexagonal-shaped room cut in half, the medical building a converted Victorian. The psychiatrist begins by asking questions in that lovely tenor voice. I picture him as a child singing in a choir, ears shining, face lifted, eyes scaling the altitude of vaults above him.

"Has the homework gotten easier for him . . . good, good . . . How about mood? Is he more flexible?"

I listen while Guy describes the closet scene. I distract myself by trying to remember the Greek and Latin roots of applicable words. *Pharmakos* means "poison" as well as "medicine." Then I break in.

"In what way is this supposed to be easier?" Both men look at me quizzically.

"Well, the teacher report indicates that there are fewer performance issues at school. But you're right. It takes a while to calibrate these things."

I wonder if calibration accounts for the increase in categories of mental disorder—I looked that up, too. In 1952 the Diagnostic Psychiatric Manual listed 106; now there are close to 400.

"We want to give this a fair shot," says Guy. "We don't want obstacles for Norman."

I feel a distinct urge to sock my husband.

"I can speak for myself," I say. "What are the chances of this whole thing wearing off? Of him growing out of it."

"Speaking in terms of percentages, the estimates vary widely. The number of children diagnosed with ADHD who continue to have problems has been estimated from 30 to 80 percent."

"Huh, that wide a range," says Guy. I shoot him a look of victory, but Guy is keeping his eyes on the doctor.

"You know," says Guy, "when I was a kid, I was a lot like him. I scrazzed around and drove my parents nuts. And the teachers said the same things. Lots of potential if only he would apply himself. We didn't have anger-management groups back then, just sadistic nuns."

I feel my eyes stinging with the abrupt return of love. Guy will do the right thing. We will love Norman through this.

The psychiatrist leans forward over his knees and clasps his hands. "Diagnoses aren't that important. Norman could very well grow out of this, but what's important now is that he feel successful in school and with his peers."

"I agree," says Guy. "We'll stay the course."

"How about you, Maeve?" asks the psychiatrist.

But I am fixated on the therapy toys—wooden pizzas and mini-ambulances—as my face crumples up like a piece of paper.

Guy puts his hand on my forearm, but I snatch it away.

"By the time a parent comes to see me," says the psychiatrist gently, "it has usually been tough for a long time."

But it isn't sorrow that I feel as the tears pump forth, it's rage, pure unadulterated rage, at what I can't even say.

I am the first one out the door and into the waiting room. I find Norman tearing a real-estate brochure into pieces, and then the pieces into pieces. I sit beside him while Guy pays at the window, watching as whole suburbs are decimated—ranch styles and Cape Codders and English Tudors and American colonials—home after home shredded. "Norman," I say, clasping his hands with my own to quiet them, "I love you."

"I know," he says, looking intently into my brown eyes with his blue.

TAKE DAILY AS NEEDED

||||||||||||||||||||||||||||||||

In the garage I find four varieties of wasp-doom—Totalkill, Home Defense, Spectracide, and Real Kill—all of them bought by my ex-husband and of unknown quantity and potency. I line them up behind me on the driveway like a mini-brigade, fullest to least full, each guaranteeing a powerful foam spray and rapid termination but none specifying how to get the contents inside the nest. I don't suppose that this is what a woman a week out of the hospital should be doing, but the overgrown lawn can't be dealt with until the wasps are dealt with, and it beats opening mail that details which procedures were covered and by what percentage. My plan is to rip open the nest with a stick and then blast the little fuckers.

The nest looks like a beat-up gray soccer ball and reminds me of the pictures of a self-sealed tumor that a cancer survivor once showed me. Whenever I want to cheer myself up, I say to myself, *At least you didn't get cancer.* Only vague autoimmune diseases such as lupus or Crohns's or ulcerative colitis, incurable but manageable. The doctors seemed to have settled on Crohn's as my diagnosis. If you want to clear a room, all you have to do is say "inflammatory bowel disease." When I told Norman the term, he said, "Sounds like flames are going to shoot out your asshole, Mom." Not surprising. When the psychiatrist told him he had Asperger's at age eleven, Norman said, "Oh great. Now I've got an *Ass Burger*. Just what I need," and he refused to go back.

I try my son on his cell phone one more time. Norman is fast on his feet—a top midfielder on the high school soccer team. His laconic "Hey" almost makes me believe he has answered. "Hey, I'll check my messages probably weeks after you call, and if you've said something witty or worthwhile, I'll call back." What? Am I supposed to appreciate his candor or call him an arrogant little punk ass?

I tear at the nest with abrupt vengeance, dropping the stick and ducking my head as I send the foam spray toward the wasps, which look like agitated jelly beans. A few fly at me and hover about the trap door trying to return to the colony, and I zap those too. The chant in my brain hisses its own stream of invective: *Die! You little fuckers! Die!* The cloud that roils over my head smells like industrial solvent and Jean Nate Eau de Toilette. I run from the toxic lemony mist, pulling the garage door down with a strength I didn't know I had. Holding myself against the washing machine, I allow myself to cry for about one minute . . . because who could you ask to do this favor? Who? And I myself am so full of chemicals—chemicals that weaken me, chemicals that sustain me.

SIDE EFFECTS: Dizziness or stomach upset may occur. Tell your doctor immediately if you experience yellowing skin or eyes.

On Monday morning I post an ad with the Center for Student Work Experience at the local college. In my day it was simply called the Job Board.

Six calls come in that afternoon, and I pull the ad before the phone can ring again. I take the first candidate because he sounds eager and organized. "Be there at 4:00." When his shaved head comes bobbing up the driveway, my first thought is that I've hired a skinhead.

He walks with a springy step, a bend and lurch motion that conveys energy to spare. When I open the door he smiles at me, the width of his untrained teeth spread in a cheery overbite, making a valid case against orthodonture. He ducks his head slightly as though in deference or modesty, and it's then that I realize my lilac pajama bottoms are sticking out from beneath my coat. Well, I'm up, at any rate—got my hair combed and my lipstick on but forgot about the lower half.

His forearms are speckled with paint, and I focus on the splotches for a moment as though they were a dot-to-dot I could complete. "Good afternoon," he says, "I'm Wesley Eastman." I am surprised by the span of the hand he extends to me, his slender thumb long enough to touch the underside of my wrist.

"Yes, ma'am, I'm studying at the community college."

"Please, call me Maeve."

He smiles that beamy smile again, and his eyes are a warm, loamy brown. I like him. I don't have to decide I like him. I just do.

"You know five people called right after you did. I took the ad off-line."

"I don't doubt that," he says. "My friend showed up for a dish-washing job at Speedy O's and there were thirty people there."

"Hard times. I need to fix this place up and sell it. Too much for me to maintain."

"Gotcha. I just moved my mom in with my aunt, now that she's done with her deadbeat boyfriend, and my girlfriend just moved in with me. This recession ain't all bad."

I nod. "My son lives with me. He's fourteen. And my daughter, who's ten." I shrug, as if that's all there is to say. I do not want to talk about my pending divorce. You don't tell strangers that you are a woman living alone.

"Oh man, I gave my mom hell at that age."

"Yeah? I read that boys at this age have seven testosterone surges a day. I swear I feel every one of them."

"You got that right." Wesley laughs then ducks his head again in that little gesture of deference. "Your ad mentioned some home repair."

"Yeah, my son punched some holes in the house. But there's outdoor work, too."

"Did he break any fingers?"

"Nope, but he did feel bad later. Hardheaded and hard knuck-led, I guess."

I'd come close to calling the police the last time Norman lost his temper, but I knew too much about what could happen to kids when an At-Risk Youth Petition was filed. There was no guarantee I could get Norman back out of the system once he went in. Instead I called his father.

"Why don't you show me the outside repairs first," Wesley says, taking a step back and opening his broad hands toward the yard, inviting me out since I had yet to invite him in. "Is it okay if I park my truck there?" He motions toward the brown beater Datsun parked at an incline across from the neighbors. There's a snowflake fracture in the windshield, and the hood looks like too many people have sat on it.

I shrug. "I don't see why not."

"I have to park my truck facing downhill cause the starter is broken."

He explains to me how he can save me the expense of replacing the front boards on the house by cutting off the eave ends and sealing them. He isn't sure about the garage; he needs to see the other side of the door. He follows me through the laundry room and stands looking up at the tracking for the door. I turn toward the machines, embarrassed. When my ex-husband moved out, he left a sign taped to the dryer, black block letters in Sharpie pen. It reads, "Clean the Lint Tray Every Time You Use the Dryer." His last stand for order. I step over and tear it off. Oh, the petty faults that had ticked throughout the day. I did clean the lint trap, only I liked to wait until the lint was thick, until I could roll it up in my hands like a blanket.

Then I notice that above the dryer, taped to the utility cupboard, is the map of the garden my mother-in-law made after a summer visit: hydrangeas in a circle around the birdbath, azaleas and forsythia in the back where screening was needed. Another plan I was supposed to carry out. I tear that one down, too.

Wesley is waiting for me to turn around. "Looky here," he says.

He pushes his thumbnail through the panel that meets the driveway. "It's rotted through for sure." Black mold stripes the garage door three panels up.

"Check it out," he says, leaning closer. "It's sprouting wee little mushrooms."

This strikes me as very funny, even though I'm going to have to put a garage door on my credit card if I ever want to sell this place. That along with charges for propane, prescriptions, and snow tires. "Wee little mushrooms," he says again, "for real."

Back outside, he squints up at the roof. "Power wash and clean the gutters. Okay. I should be able to bust that out by Thursday."

I can tell he's a find as handymen go—honest, resourceful, and ready to save me money. I decide to show him the broken bathroom fan. He stands on the toilet and turns the fan with his fingers.

"Heck," he says, "this don't need replacing." He blinks to get the crud out of his eyes. "This just needs a good cleaning and some WD-40."

"WD-40 will fix everything," I say, caught up in the spirit of the moment.

"Straight shootin' it will. Get a stuck wedding band off with that stuff."

He smiles down at me from atop the toilet, a purely friendly smile, but clearly he has missed nothing. Then he steps down without so much as a hand to steady himself. As I stand beside him in the cramped space of the bathroom, I feel the heat his body emanates, and I have the urge to turn and round my back to him as I would sitting before a fire, letting my muscles go.

We sit at the kitchen table and make a list of supplies he will pick up. I don't know if I should write him a check or give him cash, and a little voice in me questions the prudence of doing either.

"Something you should know about me." Wes says. "I've been clean and sober for three years. I won't flake out on you."

"Good for you," I say, surprising myself by adding, "though I can think of a lot of reasons to drink."

"It is done unto you as you believe."

"Who said that?"

"Christ . . . somewhere."

"Oh," I say dully, wary that Wesley might now produce a Christ quote at every turn.

"A patch kit," he says, clicking the button on the pen.

"A patch kit?" I pick up one of the five orange vials on the table and turn it until I hear the pills inside tilt.

SIDE EFFECTS: *Easy bruising, bleeding, unusual tiredness, shortness of breath.*

"For those divots your son made in the walls. I'll fix a little mesh to the drywall first because them holes are too big for Spackle all by itself. You want me to teach him? Cause maybe he should know how."

"Oh," I say, picturing Norman turning away from me and punching another hole and then another, tears smarting in his eyes. "No, he's at his father's this week. But thanks."

I don't tell Wes that my son moved out a week ago, over to his Dad's. Norman and I have fought so much since I got sick. I read the pamphlets on chronic illness and living with children. Supposedly, if you assure them that all you need is some extra help or extra rest, they will respond in loving, reasonable ways. This is not true at my house. My children want to incite the wolverine in me; they want me to come tearing out of my den, teeth barred and ready to fend off wolf packs, cougars, and grizzly bears. In other words, they're not reassured that I'm okay unless there's a daily show of force. And everything I ask Norman to help with only seems to piss him off further. Meantime, his poor sister is hiding in her room, or lying in my bed reading aloud to me from her schoolbooks.

If Norman's father asked him to do the dishes, it would be about the chores. With me, it's about being controlled. It's about his autonomy versus my will. It's about useless repetitive female tasks. Norman is angry at himself when he cooperates because that means submission, but he's also angry at himself when he bullies me because that's domination. He's also angry because he can't articulate any of this.

35

I can't win and I can't break free, and since I came home from the hospital, I simply don't have the strength to devote myself to domestic combat even if it is the only means of reassuring him that I will be okay, even if I'm not sure that's true myself. It's hard to get well around a perpetually pissed-off person.

When he came back to the house to get his guitar amp, Norman told me, "Moving to Dad's is like being a fucking Vietnam vet and stumbling into a Buddhist temple."

I did not say, "Hardly." I did not say, "At least I'm not a crackhead mom." I said, "I'm glad you feel peaceful there," and for that I was rewarded with a brief hug.

My son is right on some level. You have to love a monster to love an ambitious woman, a woman who wants to have some effect upon the world, a woman who feels some days like she has eight arms, eight legs, and snakes growing out of the top of her head. Before the divorce I decided I wanted to be more than a court-appointed mediator. I wanted to be a paralegal in a progressive family law firm, preferably one dedicated to collaborative resolution, which really would only be an extension of what I was already doing. So, in addition to my regular job, I started taking paralegal classes at night at the local community college. My husband wanted to know why I couldn't be content, and I wondered it myself. Maybe because I wanted some say in who my clients were, not like the last ones stuck in my memory bank—the mother who refused to disclose how much erythromycin she'd given their daughter when it was the father's turn for visitation.

"She's a fucking psycho bitch," the father blurted in the family-friendly lobby of the Dispute Resolution Center.

The mother turned to her daughter and said, "Don't worry, honey, Daddy just has a temper problem."

The father looked to me for sympathy. "Every day I would love to tell this woman to get off her fat, lazy ass and show her daughter what responsibility means, not how to live off everyone else."

This was the content of my work: Everyone had a bitch or bastard who was 100 percent evil. If you thought up the worst thing you could say about somebody and applied it, that was the person you were divorcing. It was my job to lead away the child clutching her Miss Kitty purse—her parka smelling of nicotine and cat pee, hair falling in blonde ringlets that won't last. She would have to be interviewed separately, and usually what the child said could restore the parents to reason; otherwise it was off to trial and the imperial impatience of a judge who'd seen it all and too much. It was my job to say to the parents, "No, you're not coming in with her." That's where most of the manipulation ended. And it was my job to remind the parents that hurling unfounded accusations was called perjury in front of a judge.

What I wanted in my career was to operate on good faith at least some of the time, with people who could keep the best interests of the child in mind at least some of the time. And I did want to make more money, for Norman and Noelle's futures, because their father and I hadn't saved a cent toward college or training, whatever it might be—and Guy's idea was to take a second mortgage out on the house while mine was to roll over our retirement and put it into a paralegal degree. We argued over the children's future constantly and, in so doing, shredded it.

Hair loss may occur during the first few months of treatment.

I saw the women who weren't like me—at soccer, at parent night. They yawned in the afternoons instead of downing Starbucks double shots cold from the can. They wore toe rings, painted nails, diamond solitaires, little hoodies and stringy tank tops like their daughters, or else they'd desexed themselves, wore fumigator's tents and bowl cuts. I could understand why I tired Guy out. I had been known to make a potluck contribution in the trunk of my car—ripping open two bags of frozen meatballs, dumping them into a crockpot, and asking the hostess to plug it in immediately.

The day Norman left for his father's, he wouldn't look up from the screen where hairy neon-purple cockroaches, bloated and writhing, waited to be shot, zapped, powed, and then melted into undulating violet protoplasm that changed color like a giant mood ring. Were these the images that inhabited my son's mind? Apparently. In the hospital support group they told me to create a metaphor for my illness.

Instead of yelling, "Turn that goddamn thing off," I said, in my American Medical Association parent-approved voice, "Five-minute warning. Then it's time."

"But Mom, I almost beat the next boss."

"It doesn't matter," I said. "Dinner is almost ready."

"I finished chopping the carrots," Noelle called from the kitchen.

"Thank you, sweetheart," I said.

"Why doesn't he have to do anything?"

"He'll do the dishes," I said. But Norman hadn't turned his attention from the game. "Did you hear that, Norman?"

"I just want to get to the secret chamber. Aww shit," he yelled. He'd missed the yellow, tail-torqueing lobster that coughed radioactive Brillo pads, and evidently it was my fault. And this was one of the mild games, not the survival-horror-war genre. To my son's generation, unless they have a relative fighting in Afghanistan or Iraq, the war is just another game, and the tag line always reads, "Join the party as battle ensues!"

On the Sunday Norman moved to his father's, I asked him to turn his video game off.

"Get out of my room," he said, eyes fixed upon the blaze inside the monitor.

"Your five-minute warning is over."

No answer.

I leaned on the doorframe. The room was bending around me like a carousel night-light. *This medication may cause dizziness, fainting.* On Sundays Norman was obligated to do two household chores—he could choose.

I knocked on his door again even though it was open.

"Go away," he yelled. *Increase in blood pressure. Persistent fever, chills, shaking, masklike facial expressions, muscle spasms. Take daily as needed.*

"I do not deserve to be treated this way," I yelled back as the door slammed in my face. "Nothing has changed about the chores around here."

I lay down on the lumpy futon couch, tilting leeward with it, my guts sloshing about in my ears. I could see myself in the picture window of the family room; a longish, pinkish form looking like a hot dog in a bun. *Okay*, I said to myself, *last time*, and I hauled myself to my feet.

I knocked.

"Leave me the *fuck* alone," he yelled.

My hand turned the knob reflexively. Locked.

"You open this door, Norman." The tiny little AMA parent-approved voice whispered at me: *You can choose to walk away while you're still calm.* I took a breath. "I know you're mad about the divorce, but you need to open this door."

"I'm only mad because you and Dad won't fucking stop talking about it."

"Norman, I'm sick. I need your help."

"Wah wah wah."

That did it. I picked my key ring up off the table. It had a straight metal poker on it that sprung the latch of the lock if I put it into the hole at the center of the knob.

The door sprung open, and Norman jumped to his feet. As fast as I could snap my fingers, he was in the doorway, close enough that I could thump him on the chest.

"Stay the fuck out of my room, you manic bitch."

I looked up at him very deliberately before I slapped him, this man-child towering over me. "No one calls me that," I hissed at him. "No one."

His eyes watered, but he held very still, not taking a step back.

"I'm going to call your father." The fingers of my hand burned.

"Go ahead. That's what Dad thinks of you, too."

I turned on my heel and headed down the hall to my room. I found myself gasping for air, as though I had fallen overboard and slapped against the water. How could it be that the boy I loved most in the world—my own, dear, tender boy—could turn into a rendition of my worst boyfriend, could treat me in a way I'd long ago decided I'd never stand for.

Guy was kind when I stopped crying long enough to call him. "Maybe it's time for Norman to come and live with me for a while."

"I'm sick," I said, as though newly discovering it. "I'm sick."

"You pushed yourself too hard."

Every time Guy attributes my illness to stress, I bristle. The words *manic bitch* come to mind. "You think you're being sympathetic, but really all you want to be is right."

"Jesus, I was only trying to be helpful."

"I wanted to get ahead. But that would have required you to do more."

"We're not going there, Maeve. We're not."

My face and feet are suddenly warm. *You couldn't have handled it*, I think, *if I'd out-earned you.* But that's over now. Its pointlessness makes me want to lie down. *Increased sweating, sensitivity to heat, mental/mood changes, vomiting.*

On Tuesday morning I return from an epic marketing trip, epic for me anyway, and see Wes up on the roof, nails in his mouth. He is astride the house, appearing to ride it as the fir and cedar trees behind him sway. When I cut the engine he looks down, and we wave. "Ahoy, matey," he yells.

I smile but don't yell back. Conserving energy is a new lesson I practice daily, so I won't run out of energy before the practicalities are taken care of.

I had asked the checker to load the bags light, since Noelle is at school, and I find that he's turned a frozen pie on its side and stuffed a frozen pizza behind it. These are the offerings I intend to make to Norman if he ever comes back. Now I turn the pie flat and carry the bag against my forearms into the kitchen.

"Hey," I hear Wes call from the door. "Mind if I step in."

"Okay," I say, and then he is standing there, dangling two canvas shopping bags from each hand.

40

"Wow, thanks," I say, shoving the coffee pot back to make room. "Why don't you put them here."

He cocks his head sideways so that our eyes meet. "You sound low," he says.

He reads me with such accuracy, I wonder what I must look like or sound like.

"I'm sick," I say, that phrase I can't get used to. "I mean, I'm on medical leave." I gesture toward the vials of pills on the kitchen table.

"My mom's got hep C."

I look at him blankly. Is this some new disease?

"Hepatitis C," he says gravely. "Oh yeah, I know a whole bunch about chronic illness."

"Well, I got a bad one."

"It'll get easier to deal with," he says. "Think of yourself like a race car. You're in the pit now and the team is working on you, but you'll recalibrate your life, and you'll be good to go."

"I like that. I'm in the pit now."

"But you'll get out of the pit," he says, wagging a finger. "Hey, I need to leave early tomorrow afternoon."

"Not a problem. Like I said, this job can fit around your schedule."

"Well, it's kinda special. We're having a party. My mom and me, we're celebrating our recovery date."

"That's neat, that you chose recovery together, that you can hang out together."

I remember asking Norman to clean up his room before the appraiser came. *Are we going to move?* He was stricken, fear flaring his nostrils, his face suddenly flush.

I like looking out the family-room window in the afternoon. Now that Norman is at his father's, I take naps on the couch. The backyard is giving up its boundaries, turning back into forest. Goat's beard hangs like great swaths of lace beneath the firs, and the huckleberries make a foreground of red dots against the sword ferns. I am drowsing in a luxuriant sleep when the phone rings.

"Mom, can you loan me some money or buy me a pack of cigarettes?"

"Honey, you can't smoke and survive soccer drills."

"I don't care about the team anymore. And I'm not smoking cigarettes anyway. I just need some money."

"What's the deal, Norm?"

"I want to buy some pot, Mom, if you must know."

"That's not going to fix things."

"Yes it will. You have no idea how dark I feel. I hate myself. I hate every minute of every day. The only reason I have for existing is to smoke pot."

"Norman, I understand that you feel extreme right now."

"No, I feel beyond black. I'm where black melts."

"Is it school? Norman. Is it the team?"

"I don't know, Mom. Everything sucks. I mean, yeah, I'm sick of hanging with jocks and school is ridiculously cliquey, and when I go over to friends' houses their parents look at me like I'm going to steal their big gold crucifixes. But it's beyond that. I can't see any purpose to anything. It's like I'm behind Plexiglas watching all these stupid little fucking gyrations and I can't relate, at any level."

"Honey, it's not going to be like this forever. If high school is wrong for you, we'll find a better match. You can do Running Start. You can go to community college. Skip high school if you don't respect it. This isn't your whole life. You're not stuck."

"Yeah, but that means you've got to care about the future, Mom, and I honestly don't, Mom. I don't."

"Depression can be treated, son. We've talked about this."

"Don't even speak to me in that pseudo-psychiatrist voice. You and Dad can take all the pills you want."

"Son, there's family history to consider—"

"I don't want to be fuckin' treated, Mom. I don't even want to *be*."

"Promise me, Norman, promise—"

"No, Mom, I'm not promising you anything." All I hear after is the flatline of the dial tone.

While other parents talk about colleges and scholarships, my goal for Norman has always been *twenty-five and alive*. I say this like a chant now, to keep myself together while I search for my purse and keys. *Twenty-five and alive*.

Guy meets me in the parking lot of his apartment building. He's wearing the green, thin-wale, corduroy shirt I bought for him last year, and I notice that he has cut his hair very short—that new-again 50s look, the almost crew cut in middle age. He wears it well because his features are angular, beaky.

"We can call for a crisis responder or take him to the emergency room," I say as I come up beside him.

"Whoa," says Guy. "Let's just see where he's at."

We take the stairs together, and I am grateful that one of us isn't having visions of Norman hanging from the end of his belt.

We burst in like a SWAT team, and Norman looks up from his guitar, wide-eyed on the sofa. "Jesus," he says as though we are the ones who scared him.

RARE BUT VERY SERIOUS SIDE EFFECT: trouble breathing.

Guy walks me to my car afterward. "Norman has been upset about a girl, a new girl at school. She broke it off with him. I haven't had time to tell you."

"Okay. Well, maybe it's a delayed reaction too, you know, to the divorce proceedings." I slip into legalese without meaning to.

"I certainly wouldn't be the one to say it," he chuckles awkwardly, "but that's a large part of it, I think."

I say nothing and exhale heat through my nose. We are talking across the roof of the car while I hold my door open.

"Listen," he says, his tone softer. "I'm not going to file even though the waiting period is over."

"But—"

He waves his hand in the air, erasing what I am about to say. "You don't have to say it. I know you're not coming back."

"So, what are you saying?"

"I just want you to have health insurance until you get out of this . . . this thing."

"Oh, Guy, that's huge." Tears prickle my eyes.

He breaks my gaze and looks at the hood of the car, then taps on the roof once. "I've gotta go."

I pull out of the driveway, past the vine maples whose leaves are backlit and showing all their veins. The light between them stabs at my eyes like showers of sparks. It seems that Norman has gotten what he needed—both of his parents, there with him, in mutual compassion. Yes, the kid threw away his meds again, and we've been advised to hide all ours, but Guy surprised me, telling Norman, "Okay. We'll try things your way for a while. Say pot is your medication, and you're not going to stop smoking it. But then you've got to use it like medication, and not just party." It was brilliant of him, really. Here I had been fighting Norman tooth and nail over getting stoned. All this partying was going to cost him his position on the team if he didn't watch out.

"Look," Guy said in the parking lot. "Pot may be one of the things keeping Norman alive right now. If he gets kicked off the soccer team, so be it."

These were the moments with Guy that had always brought me back into the marriage—his compassion and common sense as a parent had seen us through the worst.

I am still stunned sometimes by the enormity of my decision to leave him. We were, after all, educated people who married believing we were equals, feminist men and women, embarking on a great and noble experiment. We never imagined that fifteen years of full-time work and parenthood would leave us almost no resilience at all, and that the shortfall of energy would become a deficit in sympathy. In desperation, we turned to counseling and doctors, where each of us soon was diagnosed with all variety of disorders—cyclothymia, dysthymia, mania, generalized anxiety disorder—and a smorgasbord of presenting traits. We'd learned the language of specialists; diagnoses had replaced epiphanies. The medicine cabinet had filled: Zoloft, Celexa, Elavil, Ativan, Wellbutrin, BuSpar, Restoril. Like the moon- and star-shaped marshmallows Norman sifted from his breakfast cereal, his parents swallowed blue ones, pink ones, yellow ones. And then it was Norman's turn. And Norman was refusing.

I come home from errands Wednesday and find Wes pressing blue painter's tape around the molding in the family room.

"This is the room you wanted painted, right?"

"Yes."

"Your kid stopped by today."

"Did he say what he wanted?"

"Yeah, he came by to get his guitar pedal. I says fine with me and he stomps out."

I look up at the 1973 ceiling, which has come to look like a bad rash—raised hives blotchy everywhere as though the house has had a bad reaction. I stand there with the car keys in one hand and my purse in the other, feeling my eyes brim with tears.

"Whoa, whoa, whoa," says Wes. He wipes his hands on a rag and steps in front me. My purse and keys drop. I'm babbling about Norman.

It isn't just a hug that Wes gives me; he encloses me so that I can lay my head on his shoulder and weep. Up close I notice the scrunched folds at the back of his neck. When he feels me straighten, he steps away.

"Hey, your kid won't be a hellcat forever. Man, I think of all the shit I flipped my mom."

"Good," I say, my voice thick with mucus. "I'll be so happy when we're past this."

"I don't know if you're the praying kind," Wes says, watching me shake my head, "but I am, so I'll pray on it for you."

"Thank you," I say. "I need all the help I can get."

At the gastroenterologist's the following morning, I flip through some women's magazines and read "What Not to Do the Morning After." The article advises staying for coffee but not for breakfast, and making an excuse—"I've got a brunch date." Why do they always recommend lying? Is that the way to ensure that you get married, to take up a life of lying? I know you can't be in charge of someone else's change, but what does it say if you can't reveal your own? Did marriage mean you couldn't have goals unless the other party approved, and wasn't that the Overwhelming Compromise? The one that set up the constant grinding accountability and resentment between you?

SIDE EFFECTS: *Decreased sexual ability, enlarged painful breasts, unusual restlessness.*

There was such a gulf between what I once thought was possible when I first married and what took hold increasingly—the notion that someone was in charge. Creeping paternalism. How confusing when Guy talked like a feminist but harrumphed and galumphed if the domestic routine was altered in any way. I remember being afraid to tell Guy about a dent in the car. Should I have laughed in his face? When did it stop being about taking turns? Where was the line between sacrifice and surrender, the one an action, the other one's entire being?

When I pull in the driveway, I see Wes on the ladder at the butt end of one of the eaves, his back arched, the eave only inches from his chest. I don't call out or wave. Norman is standing at the bottom of the ladder. I sit very still, listening to the fan of the engine cooling itself and their voices floating over the sound.

"Hey, man, can I bum a smoke? Not to be a total hobo or anything." Norman smiles at this last bit. His smile is quick and winning; he has no idea how beautiful he is.

"Tell you what, bro, take this paint, and I'll smoke you out when I'm done."

I watch as Wes lifts the paint can and lowers it to Norman, who receives it with both hands.

"Okay," says Wes, coming down. "Now I go roof monkey." He repositions the ladder, climbs it, and hoists himself over the gutter. "Shit, I forgot the zinc stripping."

"Where is it?" Norman asks.

"On top of the washer in the garage." Wes signals with a jerk of his head.

Norman goes to the garage and comes out with a roll of silver metal in each hand.

"What do you do with this stuff?" he asks.

"It's moss killer, man. You nail it down so the roof won't turn green again."

"Is it toxic?"

"Not unless you lick it, dude." They have a laugh at that.

"Come on up. The view is cool from here," Wes says, taking a pack of Camels out of his pocket. His eyes travel downward from the clouds to Norman, who is clambering up the ladder. "Hey, there's your mom." He hollers down to me, "You got groceries?"

I shake my head. Norman stands beside Wes and turns toward the neighborhood. I wave at him, and he waves back. At least it starts out like a wave, but it ends up as a hand held at arm's length. In the bedroom I turn on the heating pad and lie down. I can hear the scuffling of their feet on the roof and the rattling drift of gravel that follows each step, the percussion of the hammer, and between beats—jokes and boasts and laughter. I fight the urge to sleep, hoping for a chance to speak with my son, but he leaves without coming in to say good-bye. I know because I can see him from the bedroom window, sauntering down the driveway in that pair of jeans he hemmed with a stapler.

On Friday Wesley comes to put the sealer coat on the eaves since the weather is dry enough for painting. He calls me at eight thirty in the morning to be sure I know he's coming.

"Soon as that puppy is painted, I'll start on the family room."

I see him now from the window, positioning the ladder. He's wearing dark glasses, and I wonder if he is stoned, and just as quickly I sweep the thought from my mind. Wes is not my son, though certainly his presence comforts me with the possibility of what Norman might become. Wes plants the ladder then lurches to the left suddenly, toward the rhododendrons. I get up to make coffee, like I used to for Norman, even though I can no longer drink it. Wes usually brings in his doughnut, and we chat for a while.

"Hey," he says, walking in with his dark glasses still on. "Today I'm super fly."

"What's with the glasses?"

"Shit, I got a migraine." He slumps into a chair, all pretense gone. Then he takes off the glasses and presses the palms of his hands over his eyes. I've never seen him without his good cheer.

"Caffeine will help."

"Yeah, thanks." He puts both hands around the mug I place in front of him. There are three or four creases beneath each of his eyes. "My student loan didn't come through. I wrote one of the years wrong on it I guess." Clearly, he is resigned to the mishaps of bureaucracy and complete dismissal for no discernable reason. "Next time I'll get it right."

"I'm sorry," I say. Wes is looking at the ceiling as though he could prevent the spillage of tears if he just kept his head horizontal.

"Rene is moving out. She's drinking again, but trying to make out like I'm the problem, cause we'd have more money if I dropped out of school.

"I thought we was going to get married, and when I finished next spring she would have a shot at getting a nursing degree. I've been up all night crying. Shit. My head is killing me. I'll work unless I puke again. If I start puking, I gotta go home."

"No, you should go home now, Wes. Take care of yourself."

"Home isn't home no more. Renee stole some of my stuff last night."

"That's horrible."

"Yeah." He shakes his head as though his spine just quivered. "You got any ibuprofen?"

"Yes," I say, going to fetch it from the cupboard.

"Coffee is good," he says. "I'll get my cinnamon twist outta the car."

Back at the table, Wes takes a long drought of the coffee. "Whoee, that's better. Man, I was seeing UFOs for a while there."

"You get the oracular kind?"

"If that's the word for those light thingees, then I got 'em."

"I get migraines too," I say simply.

After a while Wes says, "You gotta get this house on the market. Get out from under the past."

I shrug. "It's my boy's home."

"He'll have to man up sometime."

I watch the big bites of cinnamon twist pass behind Wesley's Adam's apple, and I know he can't afford to take an afternoon off just as sure as I know that my medical leave from work runs out in two weeks.

"You're a good person, Wes," I find myself saying.

"Yep," he says, his lovely fingers nearly all the way around the mug. "You're good people too."

"You'll find your right person," I say. "You're loving, and you deserve love."

"I sure hope it's sooner rather than later."

That night Norman stops by, like a saboteur. Noelle has gone to bed, and I am paying bills at the kitchen table. He doesn't go to the front door; he comes around the back and smacks a hand on the sliding glass. All I see for a moment is this looming figure, a pale, stretched face. The adrenalin goes straight to my eyeballs. He comes in, seems buoyant. "I, uh, I'm in the neighborhood visiting Trisha, thought I'd stop by." Trisha is a girl he's known since they were five years old and peed in the woods together.

"How you feeling?" His smile is so sudden it glints. He can only look at me long enough to ask.

My heart is pumping out pure unsaturated love, grateful to even be asked.

I shrug, waiting to see if he will hug me. He slings his long arms over my shoulders, and I go up on to my toes, mashing my face into his warm neck briefly.

"I'm sorry, Mom. I'm sorry I scared you."

"I know, honey, I know. I'm sorry I slapped you."

"Naw," he shrugs. "I deserved it. We just get like . . . unstoppable force meets immovable object. That's just how we are."

"I'm glad to see you're doing better. That's all," I say. "And your Dad too."

"You too, Mom," he says. "Good to see you out of your bathrobe."

"Yes," I laugh. "I even went to the mailbox today." Then I add quickly, "Regina came by and brought me a meatloaf."

49

"Ooof, Regina's meatloaf," he shakes his head. "Gotta go, Mom." I see that tonight he is not bearing the weight of his mother's illness, or of his parents' grief, and I want to keep it that way. I touch him lightly on the shoulder before he steps back out into the coniferous dark.

The can calls itself Orange Peel Patch. It promises to splatter texture on drywall with an adjustable nozzle, from fine to heavy. I look up at the ceiling and think, *Chicken pox, diaper rash, poison ivy, prickly heat.*

Wesley has finished putting tarps down in the family room and steps beside me. We survey the ceiling together. "Yep, you got some bald spots," he says. "We'll get this ceiling of yours texturized in time for me to start painting tomorrow."

I hold up the can. "Listen to this. 'The propellant used in this aerosol product is known to be carcinogenic according to clinical trials conducted in California.'"

"Lemme see?" Wes squints at the bottle. "Blah blah blah, BLAH, BLAH, blahddy blah."

"Like the fine print on my meds," I say wryly.

He pulls the cheap plastic goggles over his eyes, smiles at me, and lets the band snap. "Are we in California?"

"No." I raise my voice to match his.

"Does what happens in California make a damn bit of difference to us?"

"No," I shout, in the rhythm of it now.

"Then turn me loose!" He points the nozzle, laughing now, as hard as I am.

"Shit yeah!" I shout. Elation makes me tingle all over as cake batter blobs fall upon the tarp, upon the ladder rungs, upon my shoes.

In the afternoon, when I get home from the pharmacy, I again see signs that Norman has been in the house. He has put an island in warm, blue water on my computer as the screen saver—warm blue and vigorous green, shimmering just inside the screen.

THE NO-TELL HOTEL

||||||||||||||||||||||||||||||||

'm on the phone with my father's credit card company when I hear the rat raid in the kitchen. I call it a rat raid because I'm lucky if the teenagers leave me a tea bag. They even eat my Weight Watchers fudgesicles.

"So," I say to the Customer Service Agent in Delhi, "it doesn't strike anyone as odd that my father orders two computers in a row and then two telescopes?"

"Vee are just here to please the customer," the nice lady informs me in trotting syllables.

"But my father has short-term memory loss."

She speaks to me as though I'm the one with short-term memory loss. "Again, vee are just here to please the customer."

"So you calculate the shipping charges and keep on sending?"

I hear laughing and shouting from downstairs. Homer has slopped orange juice onto his toes.

"Clean it up."

"No, you fucking clean it up."

"What?" I say to the woman.

"You could have your father declared legally incompetent," she says emphatically. Evidently customer service in India knows more about the American court system than I do. My sister keeps asking me, "Where will he go when he has spent his retirement?" This morning my concerns about the homeless are more immediate. I have five teenagers in my house. I know because I counted the shoes by the back door.

After high school graduation, some kids get cards and money, presents, even cars. They get taken out to dinner. They are the ones for whom the cards are made that read, "Congratulations! You did it!" Then there are other kids you don't hear about over all the bragging. They are the ones who get kicked out of their houses and have nowhere to go. My son invites them over.

There are four of them in my kitchen when I come downstairs in my kimono with the golden koi fish on it. Mothers in bathrobes are entirely dismissible, but not women wearing kimonos. My son is slinging cereal boxes onto the counter from the cupboard above the fridge. The backs of his friends' heads look like blown-down grass, like helicopter landing pads. Apparently they all slept on my floor.

The dress code among the guys is pure Value Village: other people's tourist T-shirts (the Chicago skyline or Lake Tahoe), or occasionally a baby boomer's concert memento (these are considered a score)—say Iron Maiden proclaiming "Waysted" or Steven Tyler with his mouth over the mike. As an outer layer they all wear oversized Pendletons that can double as blankets on bad nights—pure post-grunge. Except for Carl, who is a one-man version of the British Invasion, tall and skinny enough to carry off that charcoal, stick-figure punk of the Sex Pistols. He's like a walking flashback.

By the time I enter, the teenagers are making coffee; the bitter steam emitted by the machine masks their beer-burp smell. I see rain on the window glass, and I don't want to look beyond it. June rain is the worst. The kids may be impervious, but rain in June is like sweat, someone else's. Noelle is staying overnight at a friend's so I have slept almost as late as the teenagers.

"Good morning, Your Motherness," says Sid. Last time I talked to Sid, he was applying only to jobs where persons with dreadlocks were accepted. Sometimes I feel like Dr. Phil: "And how's that working for you?" Today Sid admits that the dreads do narrow things down considerably. Beads and corks bob in his hair, which really is a masterpiece, a vertical basket, if only he were majoring in textiles. His father is on disability with L&I after a forklift accident at UPS, so Sid sleeps on the couch, and when they argue he splits. As I listen to the teenagers' conversation, I feel like I am overhearing the saga cycle of a nomadic tribe.

Sid starts in, "I come home and he's asleep on the traction board. You'd think his head would bust like a tick. Fucking pain-killer blues. He gets up and he's all yada yada this and yada yada that. List a mile long, like I'm everybody's bitch."

"Man, you are," says Carl, digging into his corn puffs with a soup spoon.

"Yeah, then my fucking mother kicks us out."

"Hey, don't say shit about your mom." This is my kid, Norman, issuing a warning. "She's cool."

Sid's mother, Tamara, has MS, and the kid has done for her since he was old enough to understand that she wasn't the kind of sick you get well from. He's a regular on my couch, but I always call his mother or she calls me, because if he's with me, I want to be sure it's on a day when the home health-care workers are stopping by.

I admire Sid, because he tries to conceive of the future. He has a plan to enter the technical college and study to be an electrician, though occasionally I question his motives. He likes to say, "It's the most dangerous of the trades. One wrong wire, man, and you're fried."

"Hey," I say. "There's sausage in the freezer. You want some?"

"Yeah, cook it up, woman." My son says this, and there's a general ripple of assent. Norman likes to talk to me in this he-man-cave-dweller diction; it makes a joke of the fact that I am still his mother cooking for her kid.

"Your mom lost it when you blew a bong hit up the dog's nose. Why'd you tell her that, man?" Carl hides behind a dark bank of hair, unless he wants you to feel his defiance, in which case he swings the curtain back, revealing eyes blunt and black. Some hurt has lingered there a long time.

"I thought she'd think it was funny," Sid says. "She's got a scrip for dope, for fuck's sake. It's not like she doesn't smoke it."

"For pain," says Homer, putting in his characteristic two words, always uttered quietly, without swagger.

"You caused your stepdad some pain all right," says Carl. "Shit, me and Norman couldn't pull you off the guy."

"He's not my stepdad. He's just some washed-up dude."

Jake is the boyfriend of Homer's mother, and Homer's house is ostensibly where they all went two days ago for a graduation party.

"He had it coming," says Norman.

"Yeah he did," says Homer. "My mother says I broke his thumb. I'll probably have to go live with my grandpa for a while."

Homer's mom would turn her socks inside out for him, give him her last beer, but Jake is her particular weakness, and together they are raising his six-year-old daughter whose meth-head mom is in jail. Managing an am/pm mini-mart is the best job Homer's mother has ever had. Homer looks like a Homer, sans the overalls. He's tall, oafish, ginger-haired, and sensitive. The kids call him Homey. His mother once offered me advice when Norman and I were going through a particularly rough patch. Patch was quite a literal reference for me back then, as my son kept socking holes in the house. "Walk the walk with him," she slurred. "That's what you gotta do."

By this, she meant that I should smoke dope and get drunk with my kid. Apparently it's not enough that he knows my politics— legalize the leaf and tax us out of war and debt—or my own extensive sampling of all the drugs a post-sixties California childhood had to offer. Babysitters came with joints, and mothers disappeared on the backs of motorcycles. Homer's grandfather has staked him to a bartending course, and I'm thinking that despite the obvious occupational hazard, he's already got a real knack for handling alcoholics.

"You guys want pancakes?" I ask, now that I've got the requisite amount of coffee in me.

"I'd be down for that," says Sid.

"Yeah, thanks, Mom," says Norman, looking up from the screen he is thumb-punching.

"Thanks, Mrs. Beaufort," says Carl, who hasn't known me for

very long or he wouldn't call me Mrs. "I hope you don't mind, but I stacked some of my stuff by the front door. My father's threatening to sell it."

I look down the hallway and see an Xbox, a laptop, and a hair dryer stacked on a guitar amp.

"That's fine. No worries."

"I'd be happy to take 'em off you," says Homer.

"Shut it," says Carl.

"It doesn't matter what your father says." Carl's waif girlfriend has appeared from downstairs. She looks at me as she speaks, and I hold her gaze. "He wouldn't even be able to figure out how to set up a PayPal account on eBay."

There's a momentary silence. Shelby has dumbfounded us all by speaking. Most of the time she just sucks on her hair and then examines the point she has made. It's quite a calligraphy brush. When she sees that everyone is looking at her, she presses her hand over Carl's. Shelby has a home, just not one that allows her to have a boyfriend in it, so she's usually here when Carl is.

"He gave you one week, man," says Sid.

"Who can find a job in one week? That's fucked up, man." This from my son, whose father helped him get a job as a busboy at a restaurant he frequents.

"What happened?" I ask, putting the sausages on the table. Neutral, that's me. Because for teenagers, even time is an opinion.

"My dad told me not to come back. He told me it wasn't my home anymore," Carl says.

"People say things they don't mean when they're upset." He gives me a quick look before I withdraw from the table.

"Oh, he meant it."

The conversation changes course, and I turn back to the pancakes bubbling in the pan. Despite how looming and loping these teenagers are, I catch myself referring to them as children. After all, they still get excited by new kinds of cereal, and they dearly love their parents—who have kicked them out, or are stretched too thin to help out, or can only offer beer, bong hits, and Top Ramen.

My own boy wears his hair conservative, short shorn, no more Mohawks or checkerboards. He's the therapist of the group, which means most of the time he doesn't have a girlfriend, although he does keep Shelby's supply of birth control in his sock drawer so her mom won't find out.

"It's like a cluster diagram, Mom," he complains. "Everybody's already slept with everybody except me, so I'm bound to piss someone off no matter what I do." On bad weeks he'll carve tic-tac-toe on his forearm, and I'll hide the sleeping pills, but most of the time he's upbeat these days, and I'm lucky I guess that he already dropped out of high school and took the GED, because he's leading the charge by being the first to hold down a job while making his desultory way toward an AA at the local community college.

After the tribe at the table has fed, they lean back onto their chair legs and stretch. I can hear the rattan chair backs straining. Two of the guys are text messaging while the others are cooking up the next plan, but occasionally they contribute to the conversation by saying, "Word."

"Are you down for the party?"

"Yeah, I'm down to kick it."

"Marina Beach, man. Bonfire."

"Did you see how ripped Joann got last time?"

"Chick would drink salt water on a desert island."

"Hey, be chill. Her mom's like mental."

"Yeah, and Homey still loves her."

"Shut up, dude."

"Shit, man, she's a mushroom cloud."

"Word, man."

"Peace out."

Sid drums on his belly. "Pancakes. Oh yeah."

I wonder sometimes what kind of values I'm imparting to these kids. I only know that if I keep this no-tell hotel running, the teenagers are less likely to run off the road or get pregnant in vacant lots. I don't ask too many questions; I just keep the freezer full of burritos and pizzas, the medicine cabinet stocked with Band-Aids and condoms, and the coffee machine prepped with filter and grind. I've heard that in Scandinavia, where sex ed assumes that young people make love, the teen pregnancy rates are very low. US teenagers have to get smashed first so that they can pretend they didn't know they were going to do it, which of course makes planning for birth control nearly impossible.

I, myself, grew up in a cul-de-sac of dangerous divorcées with just enough alimony not to care whether they were the talk of the carpool or the scandal of the neighborhood. They smoked in bed and wrote screenplays for TV or music scores for movies. They kept *The Joy of Sex* in their underwear drawer and said scary things like, "You'll remember your first time forever, so you want to make it good." A tough LA bunch, they bossed each other's kids around regularly. Martyrs to the cause of childhood they were not. "You live with your children, not for them," my mother said regularly. And live you did, if you were lucky. We had to be a scrappy bunch. Mrs. Hardeen ran over Mrs. Linde's son Dieter one frantic morning in the driveway, but since Dieter was only two, the bumper hit him smack in the middle of his forehead and he managed to land square between the tires, so no harm done. Another time, our shepherd picked a fight with Mrs. Hardeen's boxer beneath her window. Mrs. Hardeen thought to drop down the Oxford English Dictionary, volume by volume, but since she didn't have her reading glasses on, she landed one on my mother, who'd come over to break up the fight. My mother was immediately invited in for a drink. Again, no harm done.

From this childhood and these mothers, I am supposed to draw my models. They let us run the neighborhood like a pack of jackals. We rode the rich kids' bicycles into their pools at night and abandoned them at the bottom to rust. Youth is an uprising, and our mothers left us to it. Most of all, they trusted us to come out all right—scrappy moms made for scrappy kids. And despite all the consciousness raising, they kept their exes around to fix things. I get on with my ex, too, though politeness can be a detriment. You might spend a couple of years wondering, *Am I married, or am I just being polite?*

My former and I don't fight, because we text message on the big issues. When he says "don't B uptite" or "Ng. not a plan I can stick2," it looks funny on that teeny-tiny screen, as though there were a little man in there stamping his teeny-tiny foot.

Then I think about my own one-liners going the other direction. It keeps our divorce in perspective.

This morning, once the table tribe has broken up, I bring the phone to Sid on the porch, to be sure he's called his mother. Usually he responds by punching in the number. "It's all good," he'll say. I've known Tamara since I moved to the Northwest after college. Our boys went to preschool together. We watched them dance around in bugs' wings made of netting and paint on each other's tummies with chocolate pudding. We took up with each other at school events in the casual way women of a common sensibility do—Tamara, a social worker with oncology patients, and me, a legal mediator at the Dispute Resolution Center. We both laughed easily, and it seemed to mean something that we'd chosen this hippie preschool. Tamara didn't use a cane back then, though the motion of her gait was as much sideways as forward. This morning, Sid shakes his head when I hand him the phone.

"No, man, I can't handle it."

He sits in a green plastic chair, smoking. Phone in hand, I sit down next to him. I don't want to give the physical impression that a lecture is coming. Too late.

"Tell me you're not going to get on my case," he says.

"I'm not going to get on your case. I just want to know what's going on."

He gets up and paces, fingering the ceramic beads in his hair. I imagine the tenderness of some girl placing them there, or at least I hope it for him. He is looking away from me, at the townhouse next door. Someone has painted sunsets on old saws and hung them on the patio wall.

"She's always on my case about something. There's always something I'm not doing."

"She's afraid you won't be able to take care of yourself."

"Yeah, she tells me she's only here because I'm not eighteen yet. I don't even want to eat her food anymore. I've been going to the food bank."

"Sweetie." Here I can't seem to help myself. "What about your aunts and uncles. Do you hear from them?"

"Yeah, they call, and she always tells them she's fine. Shit. I wish she would go to her sister's in Oregon."

"How long have you been away, Sid?"

"Three days. I couch-surfed it at Carl's till he got kicked out. Then we went to Homey's. Now I'm here. I can't go back there. I can't."

Sid's cheeks are flush, and he pushes a few dreads away from his face. He forgets to smoke, and I'm eyeing the long ash that curls from the filter, waiting for it to drop. I recognize the T-shirt he's wearing as one of my son's: Johnny Cash flipping the famous finger at Folsom Prison. Sid's forearms are covered in an angry eczema the color of crushed cranberries. He scratches at it.

"I've got some cortisone cream," I say.

"I don't need cortisone cream," he says. There's a sheen to his eyes, pellucid as it catches in his lashes. He presses the palms of his hands against his eyelids, hard.

I pat his knee. "Sounds like you need a place to chill for a while. I'll call your mother, Sid, if you don't mind."

"That'd be cool," Sid mumbles from behind his hands, which now cover his whole face.

I clasp his shoulder as I stand up, and I close the screen door behind me quietly. I hear Norman's voice boom in the stairwell, "Hey, dude, you ready to bounce?"

Tamara doesn't answer the phone. I tell myself that she's like anybody else—she could be at the store or in the bathroom. I call her again before I leave to do my shopping in town. No answer. But it's not like I'm in her close circle of friends and know her schedule or anything. It's Sunday, and I want to market for the week. I shop at the Grocery Outlet, store of the scratched and scuffed. It's the only way I can keep the teenagers in Cheetos and

Cheerios. Tomorrow I have a paper due for my Civil Procedure and Litigation class. I call Tamara again anyway, from the parking lot, then swing out the back by the bread racks and flattened boxes.

Her house is tucked in a brambly neighborhood where the Victorians are painted popping colors like lavender and yellow; beside them, the stoops of student-occupied duplexes sag into the weeds. An overgrown weeping willow hides Tamara's front door, which is always unlocked. I knock then enter, calling out her name. Her grizzled terrier wags at me amiably, used to all the coming and going.

The house is a style you see a lot of in towns like Berkeley, Ann Arbor, or Madison: intellectual shambles—plants stacked atop books stacked upon everything else. From the ceiling, Balinese house gods fly like harpies with gold-and-black enamel wings; they hang above the scrollwork of threadbare Persian rugs. The corners of the house are filled up with dead televisions and abandoned walkers and leather suitcases, everything an inch deep in dust.

I hear Tamara's voice, muffled, as though she too were an inch deep in dust. "I'm in here."

I walk through the living room to the kitchen, the cracked panes of the French doors fractured again by spider webs and the sunlight behind them. The chairs at the table are empty.

"Tamara?"

"I'm in the bathroom."

In this house, like so many of the era, there's one bathroom off the kitchen, as though the builders only considered it one better than an outhouse.

"Tamara, should I open the door?"

"Yes, I've been in here for hours."

I open the door slowly. I see her lying on the black-and-white parquet in a periwinkle housedress, her long, dark hair caught beneath her waist. She is lying on her side; one arm pinned beneath her. The door bounces against something: her heel.

"Tamara, can you move your foot?"

"I don't know. This leg quit on me. I went to stand up and it quit on me."

She is facing the tub, away from me, but I can't get the door open enough to reach in and help her. I watch as she hooks her free arm under the one knee and pulls. We gain two inches, enough to swing the door open.

"Jesus, Tamara, you poor thing." I squat and embrace her. Together we pull her away from the tub and commode.

"Yeah," she says, "I haven't exactly had the best view from down here."

"No, I guess not." We laugh together, and I see in her face the quick-girl prettiness she possessed before the disease inhabited her. I see black scorches on her legs and on the floor, and it takes a moment before I realize it's dried excrement. The smell seems to rise as our laugh subsides.

"I don't want you to see me like this," she says, propping herself on her elbows.

"I bet you don't want to see yourself like this either," I say, reaching for the washrag by the sink and running hot water.

"No, I really don't want you to see me like this."

"Tamara," I say, scrubbing at the marks on her legs. "Do you think I'm scared of a little poop? C'mon, we've seen a sea of poop raising our babies. Been barfed on, shat on, you name it."

"One time," she says, her voice quavery with the effort, "I was changing Sid's diaper, and you know, his thing was waving around, and he peed in my eye."

"The little bugger," I say. We keep up this affable banter while I use all the washcloths I can find and fetch the paper towels from the kitchen, then she tells me where to find clean underwear and another pinafore. But there's still the problem of the leg.

"I used to be able to drag it, but now it won't bear weight."

We both stare at her leg quizzically, as though it were a busted lawn mower.

"I don't know where Sid is," she says.

It seems the opportunity I've got to take. "Tamara, Sid is at my house. He kind of broke down. I was calling and calling you. I think it's just gotten to be too much . . . for you both."

"What do you think I should do?" she says, and I can tell she knows, but she wants to hear someone else say it.

"Well, I think we should get you to the hospital and find out why your leg isn't working, and also call your family to help . . . so Sid won't feel so overwhelmed."

"He's a good boy," Tamara says, and I follow her eyes to the portrait on top of the piano. "He just needs his space right now—"

"And that's okay," I finish for her. She is leaning against my knees now, after the effort of getting the dress over her head, and I have my arms loosely around her.

"My sister's number is in the rolodex," she says, shutting her eyes. "On the hall table next to the sewing box."

When her sister Jen picks up on her end of the phone, I duck into the kitchen to introduce myself and explain the situation.

"Where's Sid?" she asks in a flat tone. "Why isn't he there?"

"Well, actually, Sid is at my house. He ran away a few days ago."

"He doesn't do enough around there."

I take a breath. "It's an awfully big burden on his shoulders."

"Okay," she says, with the tone of one moving right along. "Why don't you call me back when the medics get there, tell me what they say."

I hear the sound of Jen's sigh push through the vent of her teeth. I can hear how much she wants to forestall the moment that has arrived, and I don't blame her. At the same time, the tone of my voice surprises me. I am made of elemental substances—bone, blood, shit.

"I doubt they will be able to get her leg to work. You need to come now," I say. "It's time."

Someday soon, I realize, I will use this phrase with my own sister. When I call her about our father, I will say, "It's time."

Tamara calls for me to get her glasses and a sweater. She is thinking ahead to the hospital now, and when I return she has dragged herself half out of the bathroom into the hallway. I pick up the uncooperative limb, and we finish the job. I understand this effort. I wouldn't want to be found in a bathroom either. She looks haggard from the strain, so again I prop her back against my knees.

"Will you look at that?" she says, pointing to one blackened toenail. "Poop toe."

We laugh, but I don't move to fix it, and she doesn't ask me to.

"I used to be a sailor," she says. "I sailed to Mexico with Sid's father. I was so strong."

"You're still strong," I say. "Stronger than most."

"Sometimes I see my hands pouring all the goddamn pills on the table. I couldn't actually do it, but I see it, you know. And I begin taking them with a vengeance. It's not an act of self-destruction. People don't get that. It's open aggression, against ailment. *Yeah,* I think, *this will kill it now.*" She laughs—not bitterly, but in bafflement—at herself and her predicament.

"We need to go to Mexico," she says. "You and me. And meet us some nice men." Her eyes go soft-focus and drifty. "Mine will have this special shell that's the exact shape of my inner ear, and he'll come to me whenever I whisper into it, you know what I'm saying, he'll come to me and be my lover, and it'll be . . . it'll be . . ."

Here, Tamara just closes her eyes and makes a low sound. For a long moment I wonder if she has passed out, but she stirs, opening her eyes and holding her hands up in front of us, where they quake like aspen leaves in a fall wind.

"You know, I used to play violin with these hands. Now I can only play the sound of a siren." She drops her hands, and they land against her hips with a thud.

I hear it then, the far-off wail of the ambulance, wail without interval, that one relentless note. It doesn't reverberate through the air; it cleaves the night into dark, falling shapes.

She turns her head against my forearm, and I feel a rivulet of tears run down the thin skin. "My boy," she says. "He shoved me."

"It got too hard for you both," I whisper.

"I know. I should have called my sister sooner. But I wanted to make it to graduation."

"And you did," I say.

"He would never hit me," she murmurs. "He's a good boy. He would never hit me. He's just young is all."

We keen to the sound of boots on the drive, but I don't break her gaze. I would like to promise her something forever, this woman in my arms, but the truth is I am only a way-station boss, from this locus to the next transfer. I try to be sure each charge given to my care makes it safely, but beyond that, the train gets too small in the distance for me to see.

"That's right," I say. "He's just young is all."

TAKING MY FATHER HOSTAGE

||||||||||||||||||||||||||||||||

"Dad, we're worried. Marshall says you're going through a lot of money."

I am able to say this in the restaurant because Marie Callender's has cavernous booths; we can steer the conversation in a perilous direction knowing we will both be saved by generous helpings of pie.

"I've got enough money to keep me watered."

"It's not just about money, Dad. We want things to be easier for you."

"Easier," my father says, as though the word were soaked in vinegar.

He clears his throat. "Your grandfather lost both his legs below the knee in a minefield. At Fourth of July picnics he'd drink his fill of liquor and stagger into the trees, where he'd fall off his legs. Your grandmother and her quilting group would search the woods."

"I know, Dad."

My father looks right over the top of my head and continues. "They could hear him singing, roaring like a gelded bull, and eventually they would find one leg, and then the other." My father's spoon makes a purposeful *ching-ching-ching* sound as he stirs his already-cool coffee. "I don't think *his* life ever got easier."

I do the only thing I can do when my dad has decided to go hard-ass on me; I hit him up with love. "Dad, would you consider coming to live with me? When you're ready." It helps that the waitress shows up with our pie, banana cream for me and chocolate velvet for him.

"If it comes to that," he says, nodding, his demeanor softening appreciably. He adds another sugar to his coffee before looking up. His left hand shakes as he tries to tear the packet.

"When I get to Saint Peter's Gate," he says ruefully, "I'm going to have to ask, 'Where the hell am I?'"

Since his head injury six years ago, my father's "executive function" seems to be impaired. That's the part of the brain that governs planning, initiative, and impulse suppression. It means he doesn't follow through on things anymore, like paying the bills. His short-term memory is also impaired, and not in a small way. My father forgets to pay his mortgage, forgets to pay his taxes, forgets to look at his bank balance before ordering thousands upon thousands of dollars worth of telescopes and lenses, knives and panini grills, computers and distorted nudes in heavy, gold frames—whatever seems to be the obsession du jour. We try to make his general physician understand that these are not just senior moments. The GP responds that perhaps one of my father's medications might be impairing his memory; he'll look into it. His neurologist reports that he has passed the exams that would indicate dementia with flying colors. Of course my father has. He can summon all his ex-army-doc authority and scare the bejesus out of anyone. After that, he's super charming.

When I came down to visit for New Year's, I made him promise to take a tour of assisted-living facilities with me, and that's what we're doing today after we finish our pie. I live six hundred miles north of my father, east of Seattle, my sister lives forty miles south in Santa Cruz, and my brother lives thirty miles east in Livermore. But Dad criticizes my sister, and Mazie turns to mush and flees. One visit with him equals a major fall off the wagon. Although our father sees Mazie's alcoholism as a weakness of character, I am in the camp that sees it as a chronic disease. Mazie runs a day care out of her house and holds up fine as long as she stays mostly away from our father. Our brother is the one who bore the brunt of our father's absence as a child, while Mom sought her own happiness in a succession of husbands. Marshall would still be Dad's whipping post if he hadn't outsmarted our father on every front, but he'll never be his equal as a doctor, and he only occasionally receives begrudging admiration from Dad for his courage as an emergency-flight nurse. I am the coddler and the cajoler, the flirt and the slap, the one who became a court-ordered mediator so I could write to Dad on the Dispute Resolution Center's letterhead, though I never dare sign it anything but, "Love, Maeve."

"Feelings," my father says, almost with repugnance, "are difficult." This, from a highly trained, top-flight surgeon.

I have had to explain to my father why it hurts when he disappears to Mexico at Christmastime and forgets to tell my siblings or me. When I called his cell that year, I heard his latest girlfriend, Rayona, informing me that I could leave a message for Wendell Beaufort. I'd never even met the woman. *Hello, would you get the hell out of my father's phone?* I had to explain why it was hurtful for his grandchildren not to receive any gifts that Christmas.

"Oh," he said, abashedly, and I pictured him closing his eyes like one caught in a shameful act. "I'm sorry."

"Listen," I told him. "I didn't call you up so I could make you feel bad and hurt my own feelings. How about next year I buy gifts for the children and send you the receipts?"

"Yes," he said. "That would help me. I've never been good at this sort of thing."

When I explained the new gift system to my brother, he was furious. "That's sickening. Why should we help Dad be more self-centered than he already is?"

"Uh . . . so our children's feelings won't get hurt?"

"And he gets to be Mr. Good Guy? Forget it. They may as well know who he really is."

Now there was a question with some resonance. My father has the kind of encyclopedic mind that can drive a person barking mad. He can recite the Declaration of Independence backward, and he once found his way around Greece by using the letters he'd learned as a college fraternity member. He named his son after George Marshall, former secretary of state who conceived of the Marshall Plan and enabled post–World War II Europe to recover with American aid. He likes to quote George Marshall's famous 1947 speech at Harvard: "Our policy is not directed against any country, but against hunger, poverty, desperation, and chaos." When I was sixteen I was able to report in a snarky tone that George Marshall didn't write the speech. My father glared at me as though I were an imbecile.

"The man brought the world back from the brink of darkness. He resisted the urge to punish."

I see now that what mattered was the exemplary nobility my father believed in. When he was chief of staff at Rialto Hospital, he published the C-section rates of all the MDs in obstetrics. It didn't make him popular, but the C-section rates fell. His own crusade for the proper practice of medicine.

After lunch my father and I sit together at Chateau San Jose on a pink couch, filling out forms. Whoever thought of pink and brown as a color scheme for the elderly must have raked in the dough, because it seems to be the ubiquitous palette for sopping up tea and coffee. I write his name repeatedly: Dr. Wendell Beaufort. The care manager, Maryanne, shuts us in her mocha-mauve office and proceeds to say exactly what the video testimonials told me on the website. Fortunately, for my father this is not round two.

"I know this is not an easy decision, but so many of our residents who were unsure now wonder why they didn't do it sooner." Maryanne actually claps her hands as she says this, and I can imagine her turning the light switch on and off to capture the attention of her "learners." She is trying so hard, yet her class is failing. My father wears a scowl that grows grimmer and grimmer until the creases in his forehead bulge and buckle, forcing his eyebrows down. His lower lip sticks out like pastrami squished on rye. I smile on doggedly.

"Perhaps you have seen our activity calendar," the woman says, pushing the piece of paper toward me. "We have movie nights and bridge nights and a barber shop quartet that comes." While she is going on about the special features of Old Folksville, my father is staring fixedly into space. There's a line of silver that outlines his irises and a second of hazel that seems to have come with age; these rings give his otherwise blue-gray eyes a planetary quality. Once, when I was ten, he strapped a telescope on the back of his motorcycle and showed me the summer sky in the Santa Cruz Mountains, Venus and Jupiter big in the Southwest, meteorite showers at midnight.

"We have a bus that goes into town twice weekly," Maryanne says. "There are two shopping centers nearby."

My father could be thinking about anything—the launch of Sputnik in 1957 that led scientists to realize satellites could be used as artificial guide stars for global positioning. Because of Einstein, engineers knew to program the time-altering effects of relativity into these satellites. My father likes to say, "Einstein had a thought, and a hundred years later it proved useful." Then he smiles, fast and bright. For his whole life his teeth have stayed white and his incisors pointy, even now, when his head seems to bulge like a baby's and the circular bald spot on the back looks like crib wear.

I chose Chateau San Jose because it's built in the Mediterranean style around a garden courtyard, and they offer a top-tier option called independent living. My father wants desperately to maintain his relationship with Jing Fei, the home health-care worker he fell in love with after his head injury and the departure of Rayona. Jing Fei survived communist China and a husband who batted her around by fleeing to the States with her son, arriving with no English and no skills. Wendell helped her file her divorce papers, and the two fell in love, though there are twenty years between them. My father wants to marry Jing Fei, but she refuses to give up her Section Eight housing for a man who keeps ordering flat-screen TVs and forgets to pay the electric bill, though I am sure he is putting her son through college, and I don't care. Jing Fei is no

American princess, and she is loyal, coming each week to take my father marketing.

They fight, as lovers will. "He all the time want buy expensive things," Jing Fei yells into the telephone. "I tell him you already have dark glasses. Whole box full. What you need more for?" My father grimly complains over the phone to me, "You know that old Chinese saying? 'Work hard. Die rich?' She won't even let me buy chocolate unless it's on sale." Once, Jing Fei enlisted her sister to come over and help her break up with my father. It was as formal as a tea ceremony, but the lovers couldn't give each other up. The next week Jing Fei was back with a bag of cherries, his favorite fruit. I make a point of telling my father now, "Dad, if you get the financial thing under control, maybe Jing Fei will agree to marry you." He nods and glances out the window toward the tiered fountain. "If there's one thing I'd like to do, it's put a roof over that woman's head."

Once my father sees the magnolia trees and the hibiscus with its red trumpets, his face relaxes. We follow Maryanne, who is prattling on about floor plans. My father nods toward her backside and stops to take a few chocolates from the bowl on the piano. He thanks the Dapper Dan who allows us access to his apartment, which is filled with models of wooden boats and nautical drawings—rather nice, and some respite from the pink and brown. We decline the showing of a second apartment, giving each other the nod, and escape the ongoing nattering of Maryanne.

In the car, my father growls as I start the engine. "There's one problem here."

"What's that, Dad?" I see numerous problems; trying to gain control of his credit cards before he has spent his entire pension is only one of them.

"You don't take into account how I feel."

I hit the A/C button hard and ask, "How do you feel?"

"Like that was a boneyard." He shouts the last word, drawing long on the "o" and the "a"— "A bo-o-oneya-a-ard."

"Dad, we agreed on this together. I can only go by what I see on the website. Will you get the directions out of the glove box for the next appointment?"

"There isn't going to be a next appointment."

"I put a lot of work into this, Dad, and the next one is the one I feel best about. There's no bingo. They go to the symphony."

My father is jerking on his seat belt and swearing. I don't remember him swearing, ever. A wise and kindly bedside manner is his specialty with his patients. Pure grit stonewalling is how he withstood his teenaged kids and ex-wives. If you'd shot him with a BB gun, he would scarcely have flinched. "Goddamn son of a bitch." He gives the belt a sharp yank.

"Let go of it for a sec, Dad. Let it go." Once he is settled, I pull back out onto the expressway.

"Get into the right-hand lane," he commands, pointing his arm straight out like a drill sergeant.

"Turn right," he shouts.

I am merging with traffic and giving myself bonus kudos for remaining calm. I have never seen him so upset.

"No," he thunders. "Right! Back there."

I pull an emergency U-turn across two lanes of expressway traffic. This must be how people respond in the military when they've developed muscle memory after being shouted at in close quarters. He was Captain Beaufort.

I think we're back on track. Good. Good. Then suddenly everything about the neighborhood is too familiar. There's the Lucky Supermarket and the Peets Coffee. My father has directed me back to his condo, the sly codger.

"No way, Dad," I yell, flying past the driveway that leads into his complex. "You said you would do this with me and we're doing it." We ride along the expressway in a pit of silence.

Jing Fei is not with us today because she is at work. Not only does she work in home health care, she also works at her brother's restaurant in the evenings. She spends her one day and one evening off with my father, and for this she has earned my everlasting gratitude.

Until Jing Fei, my history with my father's women was a constant mop-up operation of leftover women who wanted me to like them so much it was painful or who called when it was over to see if I had a clue about my father's emotional life and, *Was there another woman?* There was always another woman; he just hadn't met her yet. But I genuinely like Jing Fei, who refuses to marry my father, and I suspect as a result she has lasted longer than any of his wives. Despite my siblings' cynicism I think he may have found true love late in life, now that memory loss has made him a financial liability. Jing Fei is no gold digger, not like Rayona, the married woman he was with in Hawaii when he hit his head six years ago. Rayona was American-born Chinese, but she refused to speak Mandarin with Jing Fei, which made Jing Fei livid.

"She big moon face no talka Mandarin with me. Why she like this? You tell me. She shut door to your faddah's room when she come. He sick! She no good woman. Why he no learn? God hit him in the head."

I had to agree about Rayona. The ambition of most of the women my father took up with was to get him to forget about his previous children and adopt theirs. He moved easily into new families. Each time it was his chance to be reborn as the perfect father. New families were good for that, for fashioning himself as an ideal. My sister-in-law used to exclaim, "He's like the father I never had." I wanted to answer, "He's like the father I never had either," but I never worked up the nerve.

Right now, Jing Fei is not speaking to him because he bought a thousand-dollar telescope the same day the electricity was disconnected. She paid to restore the lights, but he refused to return the telescope. "Dad," I said to him before we left the condo, "why did you buy a thousand-dollar telescope when you had no money?" We were sitting side by side in front of his computer screen, staring at his overdrawn bank accounts and unpaid mortgage.

"I don't know," he said, and his eyes welled up. My father, who believed in the value of observable fact, would not embellish even when it came to his own irrationality.

I took his hand in mine and we sat there, stunned in our shared not-knowing. Then I called my brother, asking him to transfer funds one more time from our father's rapidly dwindling pension. "Maybe Dad should take up smoking again," Marshall said.

Somewhere near Los Altos my father shouts, "Where are you going?"

"I have no idea," I answer evenly, "just not back to your place." I realize my colleagues would recommend calling Adult Protective Services on someone like me. Go ahead, I say to them in my head. I am taking my father hostage.

Our next engagement is a newly built, ultra modern form of independent living situated next to the Jewish Center of San Mateo on a campus that includes a fitness center, a day care, and a performing arts hall. It also houses a community medical library. Our guide is a young Indian woman in a maroon and gold sari with lips the color of black grapes. This cheers my dad up immeasurably. I am grateful when she asks him formally if he prefers to be called Doctor Beaufort or by his first name. "Wendell, please," my father says with a sheepish little nod of his head. *Oy fucking vey*, I think.

We walk on a multicolored earth-toned carpet past sculptures of slabbed glass. The framed art is anodized aluminum that shimmers, or huge photo closeups of plants. The apartments are glass cornered and spacious; they look out upon treetops, the Santa Cruz Mountains, clouds. The dining-room wall is entirely glass, and I am starting to feel how soothing it is to live inside a sea-green bottle. A tall slope of blonde wood delineates the wine bar, and the dining-room tables are covered in linen, each glass holding a napkin fan. I am learning: giving dignity to age is all in the details, and making sure there is still a bar is one of them. I, myself, am ready to move in.

Shaila's office has the same architectural features as the apartments we've just seen—glassed-in corners—and the effect is freeing. How can you feel cornered when the corners let out upon clouds? Pretty soon Shaila has got all the facts out of him—the worth of his condo, his dented pension, and his social security. She works it out so that he can qualify for one of the below-market value units that are subsidized in part by the city of San Mateo. To think that moments ago he was yelling at his daughter on the freeway. I don't know yet about the second mortgage he took out on the condo last year, or the other house he bought in Hawaii, or his final punishment to Mazie in his will. Shaila sketches out several different financial models.

"With this one, 90 percent of your investment comes back to yourself or your heirs. With this one, 50 percent comes back to yourself or your heirs." But then she seems to remember his dented pension and has to look up some figures.

"The option that would qualify you for the subsidy requires amortization after five years." She taps her maroon nail on a column of numbers. "This is essentially a reverse mortgage." My father looks nonplussed, and she continues. "Of course, if your concern is to leave something for your heirs, that might not be a good option."

My father looks at me and smiles serenely. "All of my children are successful," he tells her. In the moment, it feels like a triumph to hear him say this. Later it will feel like something else entirely, like his final desertion justified.

FUCK YOU! TILL NEXT CHRISTMAS

|||||||||||||||||||||||||||||||

My mother is not going to tell you that it took a disease for her to notice the little things in life—the beauty of the sunset and the fish tank and Disneyworld.

"I don't need anyone to ask me, 'Did you smoke?'" She drew out the *o* in smoke and popped her eyes. "Course I smoked. I was alive in the fifties, wasn't I?"

It was easier for me to like my mother when we both knew she was going to die. Her scrappiness, her cussedness. After her last dog died, she drove here with eight bottles of oxygen on the passenger seat, like a logjam buttressed by her purse. She was not a candidate for pulmonary rehab, not unless we could find her a new doctor to love, and that would only last about two weeks anyway. She was still cursing out the one at Chateau Coronado, albeit slowly, her words punctuated by the smacking sounds a dry tongue makes and the regular spurts in the oxygen line. "Not once did he mention that I should take a breathing test or see a pulmonologist. Not in two years."

"Mom, that's not what the doctor said when he called me."

"What did he know? He looked like he was twelve."

"Mom," I said, leafing through the COPD pamphlet I'd picked up, "there's a Let's Get Fit group in town."

"Let's Have a Fit. That's the group for me."

I laughed with her because it was true, and that was all the admission I ever expected to get, these shared moments of black humor. "Illness is not my club," she said archly, before turning her head away.

My mother and I have a complex relationship. It's not exactly *Mommie Dearest*, but it's definitely "Fuck you! Till next Christmas." We patch things up in time for the holidays, but the payback is intolerable. A week after, she'll be calling me every day when I am in the middle of fixing the kids' dinner. By the clock. Right now we're going for a long drive, but she is giving me the silent treatment. What do I care? I'm up for it.

You have to admit to becoming something of an opportunist with a mother like mine. Years ago, after the divorce, my ex had a lien on the house. I couldn't buy him out, and I couldn't blame him for wanking about his too-small apartment. He needed the money for a new mortgage. We were not happy campers; more like two people holding onto each other's shoulders while we kicked each other in the shins. When my mother offered to pay the lien on my house, I knew there would come a day when I owed her big-time, at least in her mind. But I did it anyway, so my kids wouldn't have to move and change schools. Their world had been punctured enough already. And I figured by the time she wanted to move in with me, they would be grown-up and autonomous: moving targets rather than sitting ducks.

After the doctors concluded that she had chronic obstructive pulmonary disease, she wanted me to put the house on the market and move into her tiny condo in Cupertino, California—two states away. She even threatened to sue me so she could sell the house.

"You'd better be ready to walk away from it," she said, blowing smoke into the receiver. She smoked until they gave her death as a diagnosis.

"Mom, your grandkids aren't exactly launched." The way I see it, my obligation is to the future, not the past. "You could come live here," I added, but the pause had been too long.

"Was that an invitation?"

"I don't know, Mom. I work full-time. I'll have to find out if I can take a leave."

"Well! I had no idea I was such a problem to you! I won't be bothering you further."

Describing my mother requires some antiquated verbs: huffed, rebuffed, and miffed are only the warm-up. In the end she gave me durable power of attorney for her health care, and I resorted to the Family Medical Leave Act to take some time off work. Once we got that settled she insisted on driving here by herself. Never mind if she passed out, crossed the center line, and took out a few people on the way. It was her death we were supposed to be worrying about.

The reason I'm driving from Seattle to El Cerrito now is because my mother wants to be buried in the same cemetery as her parents—Sunset View Cemetery. She made me promise to see her to St. Peter's Gate, and now it's all I can do to keep from getting a speeding ticket.

When I get south of the King Dome, I can see the Port of Seattle. The monumental red cranes that load and unload container ships look like leashed birds. Some off-ramps now have pictorial walls, pine trees stamped on concrete. Is it supposed to fool me into thinking it's not a retaining wall? Just because pine trees line the highway when you're not looking at lots for Palm Harbor Doublewides or RV Land . . . When I let my eyes travel upward, I see seventy feet of green; I see that tsunami in Japan again, that one big frothy wave busting through the tree line.

Other than that, all I see is the car in front of me or my mom's legs in lavender paisley pajamas, her shoulder and arm sheathed in a boiled wool coat with toggles, and her hands on her lap, uncharacteristically still. The seat is almost fully reclined, and her head is turned away from me. She has a face like a little fox; I swear, when's she's awake you can see her ears swivel, listening all around. Makes me remember the Menendez brothers. The prosecutor wanted to know why, after Lyle had shot his mother so many times, he shot her again. "Because she was sneaking around the table." I get it. If you've spent your life as a kid watching to see when the witch will come out, you know. I'm not saying this explains everything that happened, but mothers like these—we don't want to talk about them. Relatives always say, "She loves you so much." They wouldn't be wrong, even if they knew the goings-on at our house.

I don't have a husband to make this drive with me, and Mom is not in any condition to drive. That's a laugh. There was a time when I wanted Lorenzo to move in, but he was a high school guidance counselor and didn't make any more money than me, not enough to buy my mother out, though we did look into taking out a loan.

"If I'm correct, he has a daughter, doesn't he?" she asked.

"Yes, Mom." I had an earpiece on, and I was scrambling eggs with cheese. I was making dinner for the kids. I could hear her chewing carrots. I'm sure she was lonely.

"Yeah, Mom, he does, but she's twenty-seven."

"Well, that means that when you die, she'll be named in the will along with your kids. The proceeds will be split one more way."

That's how she talked. *The proceeds.* I was stunned as usual. But at some point you have to give up the victim shit and get to the twisty end. I turned the burner off and shoved the pan aside.

"Maeve, are you there?"

"Yeah, Mom, I'm here."

"I'm not going to agree to those terms. We need to keep things in the family."

That's what we were doing now, to my way of thinking. Yes, transporting a body across state lines without a death certificate is illegal, but the cost of an official funeral escort to California is unthinkable. I'm trying to save enough money to get Norman through junior college, and what about Noelle? My brother Marshall knows my situation; he knows it better than anyone.

He and Esme lost their gargantuan house last year, the one with the eighty-foot arch above the front door. It happened about the time white men with guns started appearing at Tea Party town halls, and we all had to learn nonsensical things, like how debts can be sold, but not ours of course. He seems blurry and muted lately, as though some essential heating element has gone out. No more fancy house in the golden hills. No more stylish highlights in his wife's hair. No more gas in the gargantuan SUV rusting in the driveway. Who names a car "Armada?" When I ask about his wife, Esme, he shakes his head. "Not happy," and his inflection is like our father's, dark and pitchy. Marshall has never escaped impossible people.

"How bad does it have to get?" I asked at Christmas, but he had his head in the fridge seeking a beverage. Mom had the TV up loud: "The Taliban has recaptured the strategically vital capital of Kunduz province in the north . . ." Operation Enduring Freedom. Who names these wars we get into? You could call Marshall's marriage Operation Enduring Captivity. Maybe that will change now.

Mazie was wrapping presents in the living room with Noelle. My sister is slight like a girl, wears blue jeans that hang low on her hips, but her face has seen hard use, the skin papery and dry from smoke. There's a flatness and swerve to her nose and a scar that runs right through her nostril. We begged her to leave that guy. Because of a felony on her record, she pretty much has to work under the table, which is why she runs an unlicensed day care out of her house. A few years back she stole her boyfriend's pain pills when she moved out. Nothing else, but he prosecuted.

It's amazing how her whole face blooms when she bends down on her knees to talk to little kids, yet with men she writes the same script everywhere she goes, always drawn to the ones who pack inner demons into the solitary confinement of their brains. When it's over, Mom loans Mazie money she knows she'll never see again.

At the bottom of Mazie's laugh is a hacking cough, and if she laughs too hard she raises her arm and puts her mouth in the crook of her elbow. While she was staying at the house, I smoked with her.

"How's Mom this morning?"

"Great," I said.

"Every major organ failing?"

"Pretty much."

To the east, Mt. Rainier rises up improbably from the flat, reminiscent of the sudden white-tipped mountains in the prints by Katsushika Hokusai, *Thirty-Six Views of Mount Fuji*. Mother would like that—points of cultural interest was another of our better topics.

Marshall is planning to meet Mom and me in Redding, not far from the state line. I may have to turn the air conditioner on by the time we reach southern Oregon. I don't like to turn her head toward me, but sometimes I have to because I don't want her to bruise up on one side.

The highway jams up at Exit 120, Joint Base Lewis-McChord. We did all right through Federal Way because I was driving in the carpool lane. Together Mother and I constitute a carpool. She would laugh at that. She and I, we do jokes together well, the ones at someone else's expense, and I let her tell her stories, the ones in which everyone else is boorish and belligerent. She has paid more money to lawyers defending her dogs than she ever has on her grandkids. She rescues dogs—that's one of the things she does—but only dogs that have been severely traumatized and are totally unpredictable. Only dogs that shake the heads of little dogs between their teeth. At Christmas we give each other soft, cozy presents—plush bathrobes, shearling slippers—wish each other relaxation with Chamomile Marigold Herbal Bath, but in the deep, in the heart, there's savagery. It has abated some since she died, yesterday. Over the holidays I could have opened the passenger door and let roll her out onto the pavement, the corners of her coat flapping back when she hit gravel. I could have watched her roll until she became a little hummock in my rearview . . . because someone else was always to blame, and children are convenient that way. Unless you've known annihilating anger, seen the reptile scales form over your own mother's eyes until she is unrecognizable, you don't get it. But today we are calm. I am calm, and she is calm. I can stand to think about the past.

Like Medea, my mother sacrificed her children to save herself. Once, she closed the elevator doors on a blind man's cane, and when the door bounced back open with him yelling, she stepped out and left me there, eight years old and blubbering apologies to someone who hadn't seen me. On shopping trips she was so rude to the salespeople that my brother and I would hide in the racks, embracing clothes on hangers.

"I can't help it that the saleslady was an absolute dolt," she'd say to our father at the table. He must have been really desperate to put it all behind him, because he took up with a lady ambulance driver he met on his rounds at the hospital, and he spent his weekends at stock-car races. You can't hear a thing on the sidelines—best of all, not your own thoughts.

When it was time to visit our father, we flew from LA to San Jose and arrived pinned with wings and laden with coloring books, all the perks of being unaccompanied minors. Mother typically left for the airport at the last minute, screaming down the traffic on the freeway, screeching up to the loading zone. "Run, run!" We herky-jerkyed down the long corridors, suitcases banging our knees, her voice in pursuit of us. More than once they held the plane at the gate for us. No wonder when my stepmother offered to take my suitcase at the other end, I replied, "No, I can carry it myself."

When the Change comes over our mother, it's stupefying . . . either way. Oh, how she kissed us in front of the pilot and stewardesses and made that girls' school wave right before the hydraulic stairs groaned into place, sealing her out.

It was on one of those car rides that she rammed all eight cylinders of her Chevy Impala into the back of a Cadillac Fleetwood, and my head shattered the windshield. Quite a while passed before she was calm enough to look at us. She was pounding the steering wheel with the flat of her palms and screaming, "I hate him, I hate him."

He, him . . . it was always our father who played the part of the demon in this fairy tale that framed the construct of our lives. He had her sent to Hazeleden for rehab, and to hear it, you would have thought she'd been marched to the Tower. Then he used it against her to gain custody, but she had fought her way back and won us in an excruciating trial. For the rest of our lives we owed her gratitude for that . . . we *owed* her. Our grandparents hovered, bought her a house up the street, sent maids, gardeners, husbands. I would love more than anything to capture her ample charm, her lively imagination, her spellbinding charisma, but it's not this that I was left with. Those things were burned away by the towering rage. When people use the expression blinding rage, I don't think they realize that Medea is not only blind in action but also in memory. The rage itself erases the deed, so that on a school morning she could hurl two plates of burnt toast across a parquet floor, screaming, "Eat that, you dogs," yet expect her children to kiss her at the school gate.

At the Kelso-Longview exit I get gas and park in the shade of an am/pm mini-mart, the furthest slip over, next to the silver box marked ICE. I don't dare get off I-5 in Portland. There are eight bridges in downtown alone. Besides, there's no self-service gas in Oregon, and I'd have to sit there hoping the attendant didn't do a double take on Mom.

When she broke down and asked if she could stay with me, I felt bad. Here was my mother, weakened by COPD, softened by it too. Or so you'd think. You try to make her happy because somehow you've forgotten that she doesn't want to be happy. You love it when she says, "I've finally realized . . ." You eat that shit up because you've forgotten that true insight would be catastrophic for her. It would require apologies, and she doesn't do apologies. She's one of those people who will say they are sorry that you feel bad, while you slip from the dining-room chair to the floor, mouth frothing from strychnine. When it comes to truthfulness, maybe little inroads are possible. Maybe. Are you looking for an epiphany? This is not your story.

Default has delegated my mother to me. Marshall's wife would have threatened to leave. Mazie is out of the running—if Mom is the witch, Mazie is the waif.

I can smell Weyerhaeuser when I return to the car, the

lumberyards and millponds of Longview—the chlorine-treated pulp and paper, the glue and sealant of laminate-wood products. The air ought to be enough to embalm you, Mother.

I notice her lips have turned a bluish purple. Other than that she's Victorian pale, although her ankles have swollen as the blood pools downward. They're the color of chopped liver. I'm glad I thought to put her in slippers.

I still feel panic this close to her in the car, and not because she's dead. My chest hurts, and if you cracked me open the way you would a crab in two hands, a gust of rank air would emanate. That's what the virtue trap will do to you. Now that we're back on the highway, I can tell her anything. Isn't that what parents are supposed to say? You can tell me anything, honey. So here's how it was for me, Mom. You'd ask me for help, then turn paranoid when I tried to give it to you. Accusations followed: I was invading, controlling, critical. The next time, I didn't try to help. Accusations followed: I didn't care, I cared only about myself, I was selfish, I've always been selfish. *RAW-ER-RAW-ER-RAW-ER-RAW.* Like a rusty crank, Mom.

When I was in my twenties, I'd try to get her help. I knew that no one would ask for this affliction. I'd tell a doctor she had a mood disorder. I'd make an appointment. She would tell the doctor I was the one who had the mood disorder. I'd laugh; I couldn't help it. Then the doctor would give me the Look. Back to Square One. I've always been such a good child, except of course when I disagree with her. Then I'm unrecognizable, then she asks, "What has come over you? You're not behaving like yourself at all."

I look to my right toward the passenger seat, and my eye does that blinkety-blinkety-blink thing, kind of a visual stutter, a permanent cower. Every once in a while my dad would bestir himself and rake the coals of the custody battle one more time. I remember the child shrink who evaluated us. My brother was younger, on the floor with the little ambulance, the police car, and the helicopter. I guess they thought Mazie was too young to have understood anything. "Children are so resilient," my mother liked to say.

The lady with the chain hanging off her glasses who talked like a substitute teacher was peppering Marshall with questions.

"How strong are you?" she asked, raising her eyebrows.

"I'm so strong," he said, "you can hit me."

"Hitting is not okay," she said. "Has someone hit you?"

Marshall was undeterred. "Go ahead. Hit me." He sucked in his stomach, and closed his eyes. A seven-year-old boy who demanded to be hit. He was trying to exercise some control here, choosing when to be hit. "Has your mother hit him?" she asked me, the younger one, the witness. Mazie was the hider. "No," I answered.

It went on for years. When Marshall was in his teens Mom would swing at him, and he'd catch her by her wrists. She looked like a rabbit then, trussed up and swinging from a pole, eyes wobbling around in their sockets . . . No, she didn't hit me. I watched. That was my job.

Mt. Saint Helens, Mt. Adams, Mt. Hood, they're all behind me now. At the northern edge of Eugene there's a prominent hummock. I remember when there was a cross atop it. The far-off hills turn lavender in the cloud light. I have to check my clock to reassure myself that we're making good time. Five hours, fourteen minutes. I can't gauge time by the light because I'm gaining light as I drive south.

Edmund Kemper killed his mother while she was sleeping and hacked her head off. Later, he said, "I hated her, but I wanted to love my mother." He was the Co-Ed Killer of the sixties, the one who put serial murder on the map. Some versions of the story say his mother locked him in the basement as a boy because he was so scary. Others say his mother locked him in the basement as a boy, and he became really scary. I understand unrelenting ambivalence, fear and love in equal extremes, no relief from it ever, just the constant vigilance. You can't say what you would do in the same situation. The sheriff commented on the brutality of the crime: "He couldn't kill her dead enough."

When Marshall came up for Mom's last Christmas, he was by himself. I guess he needed a break from Esme, a high-maintenance wife if there ever was one. I'd sorrowed over his love life with him for years, and no amount of therapy fixed it. He couldn't seem to find a woman who was punishing enough. He was there when Mom pulled up the drive, so tiny now that she looked like a shrunken head at the wheel. Marshall brought her things in while I made tea. When he left the kitchen, my mother reached across the table and took both my hands. "I don't trust him not to put me in one of those places. Lock me up in a nursing home. I couldn't bear that."

You've never felt such pathos—the ravages of a million perceived betrayals and abandonments on her face. Marshall waved to me through the doorway before he hit the remote button. TV on; Marshall off. "Mom," I said, "I love you. I wouldn't do that."

"Promise me, sweetheart. Promise."

Oh, dutifully I did, earning for the million millionth time my designation as the good child, the strong child, the generous, wise child. What is it they say about boiling a frog in water? That if you turn the heat up slowly, the frog won't jump out.

"Oh, thank you," she said. "Will the room I stay in be westward facing?"

There was my first wrong move, but it seemed to matter to her so much, and it seemed little enough to me. Marshall and I treated it as a last request, to be honored.

I carried the clothes I needed from my room to the family room. Mom was reading her *New Yorker* while Marshall dozed off to a golf tournament. Later she sat on *my* bed, watching as I unpacked her things, her lips puckering like ruched taffeta, bisected by the vertical lines of age. I heard her sigh and drop her shoulders in the same gesture. "What?" I said.

"Oh," she said, looking truly concerned. "Do you think the street noise will keep me awake?"

At Grants Pass I cross the Rogue River, grateful for the momentary roaring in my ears and the dusk that draws down over Mom's features. Years ago I took my son to the Oregon Caves National Monument. I won't go down there again, into the bad breath of the world. Norman was so excited to learn that jaguar and grizzly bear fossils had been found in the deeper chambers, but you'll never make a spelunker out of me.

At first our moments living together were only slightly off. I was in my bathrobe going up the stairs after a perfectly pleasant morning exchange. I'd gotten a book out for Mother, and she was eating a scone. As I ascended the stairs, she said, "I guess that's good-bye then."

I'd forgotten how it felt to live like this: attuned to the brittle, vigilant to the tone of taking slight.

"No, Mom. I'm not leaving for another twenty minutes. Then I'll come say good-bye." When have I not said good-bye? I'm one of those people that can't go to sleep unless everyone in the house has said good-night to me; otherwise I think someone is mad at me.

"Oh," she said, in that faraway tone of hers, eyes focused on nothing.

The body doesn't lie. That's what people don't understand. Spurts of adrenalin at any given moment, and every given moment tippy. I looked to my imaginary teleprompter for blithe, non-committal expressions—"We could do that" or "There's an idea" or "I don't mind." One day when I came home from market, Mom was squatting in front of the refrigerator.

"I'm putting these down here," she said, moving the jam jars from the door to the lowest shelf.

"Whatever you like is fine, Mom."

"I wasn't asking your permission. I'm just letting you know."

I'd forgotten this, too. Everything could be a power struggle. We needed to draw up a treaty for jam jars. Evidently jam jars needed more space between them. How could I not have known? When I moved away to college, she'd called me that night to tell me that I'd forgotten to pack my frozen food. I needed to come back for it soon.

By the time I got in the car this morning, I felt like I'd been bounced off every surface of the house. You don't know crazy unless you've seen crazy around the edges. My friend Jake is a mental-health nurse with a voice like Wolfman Jack—when he says he's had a *cra-zy* day, it means he's had to tackle a couple people, *take 'em down.* Mom, she gets skittish around the eyes like a horse about to rear, frantic but not seeing. Then who the fuck is anybody? Sometimes I am her sister, hated for her conventionality; sometimes I am her mother-in-law, inciting jealousy with my professional achievements; sometimes I am a ridiculous child who really should know better; sometimes I am her great, strong Maevy, her ever-generous daughter, her moral core.

Before the border, where I'll have to stop at the State Department of Food and Agriculture station, I smooth my mother's hair and tie a scarf around her head to obscure all but her profile. I pull her driver's license from her red wallet and put it with mine on the console. If they ask us to get out, I'll act as though I had no idea that my mother was dead. She must have died in the car. Instead they ask me if I am transporting fruit that could carry fruit flies. Also our destination. "We are going to visit my brother." When the border-patrol officer hands me back the licenses, he winks, "Mom having a little snooze, eh," and I smile at him.

Just after the town of Weed, I can see Mt. Shasta, shimmering through the scrim of twilight. I've followed the Cascades all this way south.

My mother lived through everything between October and Christmas. We went to the hospital when she caught a cold that turned into pneumonia, and then one lung collapsed. She was almost out of the nursing home when she caught one of those super bugs, MERSA, though this one hadn't been given a name yet, only a number. Back into the hospital for another week. My brother managed to be very busy in addition to being two states away, but who could blame him? Not me. By Christmas she was home and the house was full, his kids, mine, a joyous din. Noelle had won the seventh-grade Student Publication Award for an essay on the whaling rights of the Makah Tribe. We toasted her future as a writer.

"You'd think she won a presidential scholarship," Mother hissed as she set a plate by the sink. "Does she always have to be the center of attention?"

As long as I'm unhappy, Mom and I are two peas in a pod. It's telling her good news that triggers resentment.

"Jesus, Mom," said Marshall, coming up on my other side. "Give it a rest."

"I am going to my room," Mother said. "I'm tired."

I have to say, I hoped she wouldn't come back downstairs, and she didn't.

In the quiet house I took down the Christmas decorations by myself, lingering over each wool-felt gnome or lamb's wool angel that Norman had made me long ago. As I flattened wrapping paper for the recycle bin and pulled stray ornament hangers from the heater vents, Mom took a turn for the worse. The bronchodilators didn't seem to do a thing. Coughing abraded the surface of our day. Coughing, coughing, coughing. The hospice nurses came and set her up with a morphine pump, and that seemed to help: it relaxed her throat muscles some. I could hear her chatting sometimes, telling the nurse how she drove out here by herself, as though we wouldn't have come for her.

"Your mother," said the hospice nurse, "she's such a sweetheart."

"*Can* be," I corrected. The nurse studied me for a moment. She thinks I am suffering from fatigue. She assumes that I'm the self-centered one.

It's early morning, and I am bringing the oxygen bottles in off the porch when I hear my mother's halting shriek.

"Get . . . away . . . from . . . me!"

From the doorway I watch her plunging about under the bed covers.

"Get . . . away . . . from . . . me!"

I pull the quilts back in case it's the weight of them that's bothering her. She looks right at me with those eyes at the edge of crazy, and she does not see me. Next she's got her arms out and flailing—she's thrashing about like someone trying to make their way against a heavy wind. Her legs move upward and downward. She writhes.

"Get . . . away . . . from . . . me!"

I hit the morphine pump with my thumb. I don't know how many times I pump it, until the pad of my thumb stings.

One of her fingers gets hooked in the oxygen tube, ripping it out of her nose.

I'm transfixed, watching. I can still hear her voice, through the layers of inflammation, through the bubbly tissue of alveoli. I can hear the click of her tongue breaking suction from the roof of her mouth.

I go then. Past the phone. Past the refrigerator where all the numbers are posted. Outside. Up the street. The neighbor's rhododendrons are bagged in burlap. Branches are strewn upon the ground. I didn't notice that it was windy last night. I tip my head up, gulp the air. A chevron of geese crosses the low-slung sky. The clouds are the color of ash. When the V of the geese scores the shape of an A by crossing the telephone line at the far end of the neighborhood, I stop.

A is for something, I think. Not *apple*, not *apex*. *A* is for *apart* . . . that was it . . . *apart* as in not together, *apart* as in never whole.

I trudge back. Inside the house, it's quiet. My mother once told me, "Death is the final abandonment." I'd shaken my head in disbelief, as though anything so universal could be personal. *A* is for *abandonment* in her book; it is the first page. I stop inside the doorframe, thinking she is already gone, but soon I can feel her eyes in the gloom of the curtained room, and I know that she can see me. *A* is for *ambivalence*. I sit at the edge of the bed. Her breathing sounds like it is being drawn from a deep well. She whispers.

"I never asked for help in the first place."

"I know that, Mom."

"I never meant to do harm. That's the worst of it."

"I know that now, Mom."

"Did you tell people? Did you tell them what kind of mother I was?"

"No, Mom, I didn't tell." I pat her hand, and then I think about how I'm going to put her in the car and how Marshall will be there when I arrive—big and blowsy and shuffling and open-armed.

A SHOT TO THE HEAD

||||||||||||||||||||||||||||||||

"I shouldn't have shaken her like that. I shouldn't have done it."

I am in the dog park where we adults congregate after our children have been taken away by the bus. I am seeking some absolution my thirteen-year-old daughter won't give me. The dogs are falling into chuckholes left by wild geese and rain. The lake water is a spring color—more teal than pewter.

"Sometimes kids are so hardheaded, what are you going to do?"

Ivy is saying this to be conciliatory, but I know it's not what she really believes. She has the patience of Job and lives in a temperate zone all her own.

"You have to try not to get mad or you lose all credibility with them," she adds, hurling a ball from one of those launchers that looks like a long-handled ice cream scooper. Her collie chases balls, and my heeler chases dogs that chase balls, so our routine works well.

"I don't know about that," says Regina, who's a tough Berkeley girl from a Jewish-Italian family. "In Italian, it's called a shot to the head. Blacks say 'smack upside the head.' It's not like you were fighting about her homework."

"My father used to throw his shoe," says Gibran, who was born in Lebanon. "He could hook it around the corner. We lived in fear."

The conversation backs away from my confession but not entirely away from the subject.

"Right," Regina says. "We don't want our children to live in fear, but a little compliance now and then might be a treat."

"My father always said you have to show force of character," Ivy offers.

"Is that like baring your teeth?" Regina looks at me, watching me kick goose poop around. Her hair is silver and frizzy, and she belongs to that small club of women over fifty who don't color their hair. Her daughter is in college already.

"My brother once spent three days trying to make our father hit him," Gibran says, "and it didn't work." Gibran is a software designer who works from home while his wife manages an endocrinology office. He's become the honorary woman in our group.

"I guess I was lucky," says Ivy. "That or I come from really repressed people."

Down the field, my dog Tater has gone after the biggest dog he can find, a Great Dane named Samson, who is easily intimidated by persistent herding and barking. I move away from our little band knowing that next Tater will try to hump Samson. I never understood how a Dachshund could mate with a German Shepard until I saw Samson lie down on his back spread-eagle. Clearly, I made the wrong assumption about who was butch and who was femme.

I look out over the lake, wide and long as a fjord, liquid ink in the distance. If you squint at the ridgeline above, the power lines swoop upward like bridal trains and fade into the furry crew cut of the logged-off parcels. I let my eye travel over the oscillation of the green foothills. Someday the land will look less managed. Nature will strike back with catastrophic force, and the big barges of timber will no longer depart from Seattle's port for Asia. I envision millions of board feet thrown into the air: debris and wreckage shattering into flesh, into slivers, into rubble. My imagination embraces the ruinous; calamity will come to strip us bare, every one. There is an appalling appeal to it. Children knock all the blocks down and laugh at cataclysm.

My friends are talking about their children's teachers. I hear them as though at a distance, the air between us matte and hazy with weak sunlight.

Ivy is speaking. "Mr. Bosun told the kids that life is a race on the asphalt. Some run with the pack, some pull ahead, and some fall behind."

"How fucking tiresome is that?" says Regina.

"It's jock talk," says Gibran. "Winners and losers."

"What ever happened to curiosity?" asks Ivy, turning to me, but I do not chime in.

I'm off to haul Tater away from his dry-hump session, wondering if my earlier confession was too much. Perhaps now my friends feel that they have no choice but to be my ally or my foe. Maybe it is only Regina and I who feel the need to be unremittingly analytical. My parenting classes emphasized that you should never ever strike your child; if you did it was a moral failing on your part. My father had no such hindrances. He administered a swat or spank, acts that implied a parent's right to enforce life lessons. He never gave it a second thought, and neither did I. Now the Skagit Valley courthouse is abuzz with the Williams case, and the other fundamentalist parents who abide by *How to Train Up a Child*, which recommends using a switch on your six-month-old baby, letting a child burn herself so she will stay away from fire, and allowing her to fall into water so she will fear drowning.

I can understand the book's appeal on other grounds—the certainty of Michael Pearl's voice telling you just how many lashes to administer and for how long. But the intention—to break a child's will—has been around since the Puritans, and according to Alice Miller it is what gave us Hitler and a nation of followers. On the other hand, liberal parenting induces massive uncertainty, I can attest to that: judgment call upon judgment call in split-second timing.

I often refer to my thirteen-year-old daughter as Master Sgt. McElroy. She does one hundred sit-ups every morning at 6:00 a.m. Then push-ups and the splits.

"The German splits," she corrects me on the Monday of spring break. Whatever those are. Sometimes I think she is in training to hate me. She has had it with my illness, with my chronic pain. I try to keep the complaining to myself, but I am not always successful. Some mornings I take six pills and go to work. Some mornings I feel like a hubcap on the freeway. When I arrived home after work, Noelle was already in the house, though she hadn't taken the dog off the line or unloaded the dishwasher, her standard chores.

I knocked on her door, and she started talking the minute I cracked it open.

"Why didn't you text me, Mom? I was going to meet some friends at Fino's."

Fino's is the local doughnut shop.

"That would've been okay by me."

"I know, that's why I texted you."

"I'm sorry. I was in a meeting."

"It's okay. I walked to Fino's anyway, but when I got there Vangie texted me that they decided to go to her house, and I don't know Vangie's address."

"They didn't give it to you?"

"No, but it's okay."

"No, it's not. What a bunch of little crappers. Who needs friends like these?"

Suddenly, Noelle is shouting. "How do you think that makes me feel, Mom? When you tell me I have no friends."

"That's not what I said."

"That's what you said."

"No, I said—" Then I caught myself. "Please walk the dog. If we're going to go hiking tomorrow, I've got to finish my email."

"I have a headache." She lay down amid her peace-sign pillows. "Why don't you walk him?"

On days like this, my little altar to the female Buddha will do no good, nor will the children's baby pictures, nor will the stack of novels by the side of the bed, and least of all the self-help book *How to Raise an Emotionally Healthy Child When a Parent is Sick.* Even the title is dishonest; it implies a kind of distance and detachment you don't get from the bottom of the tar pit. It would be more honest to call it *How to Raise an Emotionally Healthy Child When You Want to Throw Up*. Or *When You Are Too Sick to Work Full-Time and Too Broke Not To*. Or *When Sometimes All You Really Need is Fifteen Minutes of Pure Self-Pity*. There's a chapter called "Organizing Your Support System" that instructs you to "Designate a Captain of Kindness." I could see that working if you were in for the short haul—that is, dying fast—but chronicity wears everyone out. That's the deal. Besides, how many families have reserves to offer? Everyone I know is working their asses off. Who am I supposed to call? My eighty-year-old neighbor?

I heard plates crashing together, the dog being called. "Here Tater, c'mon boy."

Later, I heard a soft knock, and Noelle opened the door to my room.

"I don't know what you're crying about, Mom, but you need a hug."

I sat up and gratefully accepted this offer of love. When we unclasped each other, I looked into her face and said, "I wish you had known me when I was strong. I was a woman who could climb mountains."

"I remember when you were super strong," she said.

How could she? She was so young, only five.

"When we were at the beach with Dad, you walked with me on your back. And when we were in Wisconsin, you always walked with us to the Tasty Freeze when no one else wanted to."

These memories were so small, not what I would have chosen as examples of my strength, but they got me up and moving, they gave me the strength to make dinner, to make a plan for Friday to go hiking.

After dinner I slipped up. I said, "I'm tired."

"You should put a sticky note on your mirror to remind you not to say 'I'm tired.'"

"What should it say?"

"Tough titty, Miss Kitty."

"No more pity," I added.

"Shut your pie hole."

"Nobody cares!" we shouted together, and laughed, and in that moment my body was returned to me as a source of pleasure.

It meant something that I was well enough for a lowland hike on Friday.

It was her spring break, not mine, and it was supposed to be fun. I got up early to answer the emails from work, and we were in the car by noon.

"Let's go swimming," my daughter Noelle said as we neared our destination. She wears her long hair in choppy layers that swing when she moves. She has the high color and copper hair of a Welsh maiden.

"Yeah, why didn't I bring my suit?" said Tanya. The two of them bounce off each other in basketball and conversation.

"Girls," I said, "our lovely sunny weather means the snow is melting. The river will be running really high."

It's April, and the drainage basin for the Skokomish River is snow-packed and flanked by glaciers. The river will be at peak flow, a thunderous hydroserpent roiling pale green with volcanic ash.

"It might be a little cold," Noelle said, her tone sing-songy and ding-batty. They were sharing Noelle's iPod by each wearing one earbud.

"Cool," said Tanya.

I peered into the rearview mirror and saw that they were bopping along to some song—their heads weaving toward and away from each other.

Three miles past the fish hatchery, I pulled over onto the gravel shoulder and parked. We had reached the trailhead of this fairly mild hike that followed the river. I turned around in my seat.

"You need to turn the music off and listen to me for a sec."

"Are we here?" Tanya asked.

"Yes." I waited while Noelle disengaged from the iPod.

"Oh, Gawd, not your Ranger Rick talk, Mom."

"No. You're too old for that."

"Yeah, Noelle, now we get the Smokey the Bear talk." Gales of giggles followed. Tanya has the jawline and lips of a super model at age thirteen, though an overbite and overcrowded teeth give her back some goofy girliness.

Noelle moved to open her door.

"That river is raging, girls. It's not swimmable, and if one of you goes into it, I'll never get you back. You hear me?"

They nodded. "So what are the ground rules?" I asked.

"Stay in sight," Noelle offered.

"Bring Hershey bars," said Tanya, whose family doesn't do much hiking.

"Good. What else?"

"Take the whistle. Carry our own water."

"Yes, but today, because the river is dangerous, I'm going to ask you not to go down to it without my permission."

"Okay," they droned.

Outside, we stood on the bridge above the water, a stone arch built by the WPA in 1937. I showed the girls the plaque. The eddies of the river glinted metallically and threw off silver darts. The undersides of the birch trees flickered in the rush of air coming off the river.

"Now," Noelle said, "my mom is going to go on about the beauty of everything." She put her hand on her hip in mock exasperation.

"Oh yes," I said as we started up the trail. "Let me begin with the camas lilies whose yellow stamens look like giant penises."

"Eewww!" the girls screamed.

"Mo-ther, how can you say that?" They ran off ahead of me though still in sight. I fell into pace with the dog.

For the first half-mile we walked along an old road paved with river boulders and bounded by willow and cottonwood, those tender trees that beavers like to take down. In a little clearing I saw a lilac bush and a crabbed fruit tree, signs of a homestead long rotted away. Up higher in the conifers the trunks of the trees were bent like pistol butts, pushed out by snow in the winter months.

As I watched the girls ahead of me—two leggy Lolitas bouncing down the trail, one cream and strawberries, one honey and dates—I had to wonder where my judgment was that morning. Noelle was wearing shorts that in my day were called "hot pants" along with a flouncy floral chiffon top, while Tanya was also clad in super-short shorts but with a lacy camisole. Why were these girls dressed for pole dancing? What kind of mother was I?

As the trail rose into cedars and maples, we talked for a moment about the color of the river—rock milk, it's called. The girls liked that, then they drew ahead again. The force of the current pushed stones, and occasionally the river emitted a loud clack, as if it had delivered a blow. We passed several smaller trails that led to the river. The next one appeared in a wide bend that promised sunlight, and Noelle waited until I was close enough to hear her. "Can we go down this one?" she shouted, and then without waiting a breath, she sashayed into the brush, Tanya right behind. I yelled "Wait!" and "Stop!" but the girls had turned into dragonflies skimming over the surface of sound. They were gone.

I charged down the trail like a she-bear until I was standing on a contour of river wash that served as a beach for two fishermen, both of whom were looking at the tender source of the initial disturbance. Maybe they were the nicest guys in the world. Maybe not.

This trail I had chosen was between logging plots and hunting grounds, a new piece the local nature conservancy had secured along the river. That was all I thought about when I planned the day: how interesting to be among the first to appreciate the new trail.

The girls were already rock collecting, oohing and ahhing over stones in their hands, bending over repeatedly to search out new ones.

"Another shitty day in paradise," the fisherman sitting on his cooler said, touching the bill of his cap above the riffled edge of flies hooked into it. His face was deeply creased, bemused. The other fisherman was bulky, less distinct in the shadow of the brush. He wore a blue shirt with a name stitched over the pocket that I couldn't read. The bulky one's glance passed over me, then his eyes traveled to Tanya, who had bent over like a slender reed. He bore the handsomeness of the deeply silent, his beard glossy and black as charcoal, his brow high, his eyes deep set. He merely dipped his head in my direction, his eyes traveling the length of Tanya's legs again as she bent over.

"Girls," I said in my Laura Ingalls Wilder teacher voice, "we need to get going." They stood up, mouths open.

"But Mom," Noelle said, "there are agates on this beach."

"Rose quartz," Tanya said, opening her smile and her hands to show me.

Behind me I heard boots on the gravel. *Grunch grunch grunch.* The bandy-legged fisherman with the flies in the bill of his cap was fetching a beer from a cooler stashed in the brush. The burly one was reeling in his line.

"Catch anything?" I asked for diversion.

"Not a one." Normally I might have chatted a bit; I admired the old sinewy guys who sucked air between their teeth and tasted all its implications for living on the land. But the colossal handsome guy in camos was openly staring now.

"Time to go, girls," I said, loudly and cheerfully. Under my breath, I added, "Move it. Now," closing down Tanya's smile like a bloom knocked off its stem.

"Afternoon, ma'am," said the wiry one, making a clicking sound after as though he were sucking a piece of toffee from the roof of his mouth.

I grabbed my daughter's arm, and she wrenched away from me, though she did start back up the feeder trail. I motioned for Tanya to follow. My arms ached. Electric signals seemed to be traveling spasmodically down the skeins of muscle. The torrential sound of the river rose in my ears. If the men came after us, no one would hear a thing.

Noelle stopped when we reached the main trail, fury bright in her eyes. A boy with his father and mother passed us. They were geocaching.

"Might be Hot Wheels in the cache like last time," the boy said.

To Noelle, his innocence affirmed the fool she knew her mother to be. Her eyes tapered to slits. "Whadya think, Mom, they gonna rape us?"

My hands bolted out, and I seized her shoulders and shook her till I heard her molars clack. She stumbled back. Color rose in her cheeks, and her eyes watered.

"You know nothing," I said, "of men," and marched down the trail toward the car, turning only once to see that they were coming behind me, all my other glances furtive, stolen like the piece of girlhood they'd lost and didn't know about yet.

Regina stays behind when the others leave; we often walk the dike between the dog park and the golf course. We disappear into the tall grass and thicket of willow up there. The sound of birds is very distinct this time of year—chickadees, nuthatches, and wrens, occasionally a goldfinch with its fleeting splash of color. "You shouldn't feel so bad," she says, picking right up on my mind's perseveration. "After I married David, we lived in his cabin, really one bedroom with a loft. Annalise and I would get into fights so bad I'd be chasing her up the loft ladder and hanging onto her ankles, and we'd both be screaming and crying, and then David would send us to our rooms."

"How is it now between you?"

"It's fine now. She brings a bottle of wine and comes to dinner."

"That'll be the day."

"It'll happen. So, what did you do after you shook the shit out of Noelle?" We are right back on the subject that matters to me. Regina is so knowing like that.

"I tried to tell Noelle why I was afraid. About the things that happened to me as a girl."

"And did she listen?"

"Who knows? Noelle gave me the silent treatment all the way home, and then they hid out in the family room and probably had a little hate fest. Where's the child-rearing chapter on rape when you need it?"

"Noelle hasn't grown up the way we did," Regina says, pointing at a branchless silver trunk rising from the marsh on the golf-course side. A pileated woodpecker has secured himself with his stiff back feather, tripod-like, and is pounding out his territory. *Tak. Tak. Tak.*

We stop to admire a nest cupped in a tri-branch. I think of the softness inside—feathers, animal fur, moss. "I had this job interview at a bar and grill," Regina says. "The boss's jeans were so ragged at the inseam, his balls would pop out when he crossed his legs. I've never been so glad not to get a job in my life."

"Fucking-A," I say, laughing.

Regina is plucking leaves off the birch trees as she walks.

"You ever been raped?" I venture, surprising myself.

"No, but some guy pinned me under a bridge once. He was holding my arms right above the elbow, and I had just enough range of motion to land one right in his squishy parts. I got away. What about you?"

"I don't know. Maybe I was date raped . . . It's hard to tell."

"Was he older?"

"Yeah. Though I had a fake ID at sixteen."

"How much older?"

"Thirty-four. He was a ski patrolman, a photographer for *Powder Magazine*."

Even as I say it I realize how odd it is that I feel the need to make him sound important. He took those pictures where the sun bursts over the black edge of a mountain ridge, turning the flanks of the north-facing slopes cobalt blue. With his camera he caught skiers in the high air above the powder. I thought he knew something pure and rapturous beyond what I felt when my skis slipped over a cornice and the sparkling clouds of powder made my cheeks sting with exhilaration. I sold ski gloves and sunglasses at the ski mountain sporting-goods store, but I longed to be remarkable; to be able to say, "I'm from *Powder Magazine*," when I introduced myself.

Drink must have called curfew on my consciousness that night because there is little left now but a few frames of memory—my head smacking into the wall when he thrust, the ache in my cunt. Afterward he said the same thing my volleyball coach said after practice: "You ready to get cleaned up now?"

"It was the seventies," Regina says. "Men expected women to fuck. It showed how liberated and independent we were."

We come to where the dike ends at a huge sandpile that the groundskeepers use for traps on the golf course.

Regina throws her arms up and releases her handful of leaves over my head like a benediction. Then she hugs me. I pull away.

"I wish I hadn't shaken the daylights out of Noelle," I say. "It wasn't the right thing to do."

"Wasn't it?" Regina says, her dark eyes ablaze. "Wasn't it?"

PACK SOMETHING BLACK

| | | | | | | | | | | | | | | | | | | | | | | | | | | | | | | |

t's mid-August, and I am in the middle of packing to go see my father. The children are coming with me, and we leave in the morning. My brother Marshall and I have planned a reunion with our father by the pool of his condo. Our sister Mazie refuses to come. Marshall and I don't try to persuade her. Our father belittles Mazie as "underemployed" because she finds value in working with toddlers. He wasn't much interested in babies after the initial pat; he liked us when we were old enough to converse about the questions of the universe, which most kids can do by the time they're six. When I try to defend Mazie, my father says, "That and a nickel will get you the bus." We don't tell him about the felony.

It's 10:42 on a Monday night when I receive the call, time enough for me to tell my children to pack something black.

Hello, my name is Investigator Garcia, and I'm calling from the Santa Clara County Coroner's Office regarding a Dr. Beaufort.

In the chain of phone calls that follow, it is established that my father has had a fatal heart attack, though we had no knowledge of his having a heart condition. He was alone and had gone to bed early. He didn't pick up the phone when Jing Fei called at the usual time. She had spent the night with him on Sunday as was her custom, but she doesn't want me to tell anybody that now. "How can he die? He walka four miles day before."

My brother says to me, "Dad's father died of a heart attack." One phone call puts forth a question, another an answer. Neither knows of the other.

In between talking to Marshall, Mazie, Jing Fei, and Regina I dial my father's number. He speaks with amazing elocution, each word articulated formally. "Hello, you have reached Wendell Beaufort. If you care to leave a message, please do so after the beep. Thank you for calling." His voice drops slightly when he says thank you. It's a wistful shift; it's the reason I will keep calling his number in the days to come until it is finally disconnected. It is the reason I will start saving messages from my children, my lover, my sister, my brother.

When we arrive at my dad's townhouse, Jing Fei is mad at Marshall, because he threw all of the food out of the fridge. They're in the kitchen, but I can hear her before I turn the deadbolt. "You throw away medicine all the way from China, very expensive, I no happy with you." The real issue is the suddenness of my father's death. My brother was thinking about the stinky food in the fridge, not the intimacy of hearth and home, and now he has unwittingly thrown away the lovers who nourished and nurtured each other. For five years Jing Fei shopped for our father, and they cooked together. I study her through the window. Her face is shallow scooped in profile, cheekbones high. She's my age, though tiny and very pretty but for the tangled teeth in her mouth.

"How come you do this? Yesterday, I thinking I have time meet you at your deddy house. I call you and wait you open, but you no come. I have key but wait you open for respect."

I step into the foyer cautiously because it is strewn with toolboxes and crockpots and rice makers. When Marshall sees me he lifts his hands toward the ceiling. Norman steps into a quick hug, and Noelle follows. I have instructed Norman to take Noelle into their grandfather's bedroom to watch a movie. He has hundreds in bins stacked all around the bed; I don't care which movie.

"Jing Fei," Marshall says, poking his head into the kitchen, "all I wanted to do was make sure there wasn't food rotting at Dad's house. I'm sorry. I didn't know you had medicine in there."

"Yes, medicine cost plenty money. You thinking maybe I just

poor peasant from China. No respect." She hasn't heard us come in; her head must have been in the fridge.

"Jing Fei," my brother says, his voice rising with the flush in his cheeks, "I didn't want the fridge to stink."

"What stink in freezer? Freezer is for make frozen. No stink in freezer."

It goes on like this for a while. Marshall steps back into the living room and starts kicking stuff on the floor halfheartedly. He kicks the Styrofoam box that holds an unassembled lamp, then a plastic bucket full of knives, a tub of sprocket wrenches. Each makes a different sound. The fact that he has just come from a Saturday soccer scrimmage makes me see the tender, tubby boy and not the lean, managerial man he is working so hard to uphold. I wander the condo, picking up this and that—a tin snuff box containing the pins my father was awarded in ski school as he passed from level to level, a geode the color of the sea—and I notice odd things, for instance that my father has three pictures of his mother near his desk, one high up on the bookcase so that she is looking over him. Or is it down on him?

The condo is worse than the mortuary. The rooms smell like an old man's bathrobe, like a closet full of T-shirts hung on wire hangers for twenty years. It intensifies as I close in on the bedroom. Fusty and something far worse emanating from a stain as black as blood pudding where the nightstand used to be. It smells like bone marrow and ham hocks boiled down to gelatin.

"Jesus," I say to Norman, wrenching open the slider. "What the hell?" For once, the children look frightened.

"Did he die in here?" Noelle asks.

"No!" I shout, though it is clear to me now that he did.

Norman looks at me over Noelle's head and nods. He knows what's what, but his sister will pitch a fit, and right now I need her to stay where she is. I throw a bathroom rug over the stain, and the kids resume watching *Fast Times at Ridgemont High*.

The chief examiner at the coroner's office told me that my father landed facedown and that the blood that flowed was not from a wound but from his mouth and his nose. The examiner explained it tactfully: "When there's a breach in a pressurized system, the liquid has to go somewhere. It was most likely postmortem." I am not so sure. I could see the outline of my father's nose in the black stain; he evidently turned his head.

Jing Fei is making big noise in the kitchen, smacking fry pans together, dropping pots inside each other. I sidle through the door Marshall exited and join him in the garage. He is examining a telescope tripod, but he quits when he sees me and gently adds it to the pile with the others.

"I'm sorry, Maeve," he says, "but I can't deal with Dad's women anymore."

"It's okay," I say. "I like Jing Fei. She's no gold digger."

"No, she'll just harp you to death." He puts a hand to his face.

"You no this, you no that," I say and get a rueful laugh from him. Then we go back to examining the astonishing array of stuff that lines the garage shelves. Boxes and boxes of outdated computers and printers sit beside George Foreman panini grills and the tall slender baskets of asparagus steamers.

"I'm trying to find the guns," Marshall says. "Before the estate auctioneers get in here and get shot by accident. I already found a rifle with a bunch of ski poles."

"Don't worry about Jing Fei," I say. "I'll take care of her."

"Thanks," Marshall says, stepping over a suitcase lying open; it's full of wristwatches. Marshall has already collected six rat-nest boxes of official papers, and he gets to figure out how to save my father's condo from foreclosure and back taxes as well as how much my dad owes in HOA fees and mini-storage, not to mention credit-card debt. I'm in charge of catering for the memorial, returning calls to his nurses, colleagues, and former patients, and showing kindness to Jing Fei, which I genuinely feel. My younger sister, Mazie, will be here tomorrow, but she will cry the whole time and drink too much. She will stay with my brother's ex-wife and remove my father's girlfriends from the picture books that I will bring to the funeral. One thing I've learned in this world: if you establish early on that you're not functional, you don't have to function. We ask little of Mazie. The flower arrangements. She gets to do the things she likes to do anyway.

I take an orange plastic bowl from one of the high shelves and hear wicked laughter. *Wah-ha-ha* it goes while a cadaverous hand in the bottom of the bowl waves at me.

"His fucking Halloween bowl," I say, turning it upside down.

"Welcome to Whacko Wendell's Downtown Emporium," my brother says, pointing to ten boxes of new tennis shoes.

I stare at an entire laundry basket full of binoculars: portable ones, stargazing ones, waterproof ones. We're trying to establish order by grouping like with like.

My brother reaches up and lifts down one of the bicycles that hangs over our heads; there must be a dozen of them, fancy Japanese or Italian carbon microfiber racing bikes. My brother is sizing up the bike to see if it would be a good fit.

"You know," I say, "I once asked Dad if he had an extra bike he could give Norman, when Norman was about fourteen. Dad looked at me, straight-faced, and he said, 'Bicycles are very expensive to ship.'"

Marshall laughs like a chased duck and points upward. "Look, this one still has the price tag hanging off of it. Three thousand dollars, and he never even rode it."

I look up at the long shelf above my father's workbench. "Hey, Marsh," I say, "maybe the guns are up there, wrapped in blankets."

"Maybe," he says. "I found the ammo under the bed along with a few court summons for back child-support payments."

We look up together and squint at the mystery packages.

Without looking at me, my brother says, "You don't want to know what's in the will."

I look back at his profile, hard.

"Not that it matters," he says, glancing at me hastily, "since there won't be anything left anyway."

"It still matters," I say.

When Marshall looks at me again, his lips quiver. "He cut Mazie out," he whispers. "Out."

When I come in from the garage, Jing Fei is feeding the fish, or I should say, the one lone fish in a huge murky tank. "Just minute," she says, thinking I have newly arrived. There's a Post-it on the corner of the tank closest to fridge. It says, "Feed Fish." The tank lights are out. In the kitchen, the counters are covered in a mix of silverware, tools, saccharine vials, and jars of Metamucil. The bread box holds electrical tape, duct tape, and translucent auto tape, the kind you put on your busted blinker lights. There are two samplers on the walls. One says, "Eat, Drink, and Remarry." The other says, "Life is Short, Eat Dessert First." I look at the packets of cherry Kool-Aid strewn amid the drill bits, and I think, *I will never meet anyone else who liked Cherry Kool-Aid, beef jerky, and a cream cheese Danish for breakfast.* Where did my father pick up these tastes? In the military? Now I will never know.

Before I came to the condo, I called the family service counselor at the mortuary, Cordelia Unzman—that is her given name. I asked her again if Jing Fei and I could come see the body. I swear to God the woman makes an effort *not* to understand me.

"You want to add a public viewing to the funeral?"

"No," I explained again, "we are not having a graveside service."

"Let me find your file," she said, as though I might not know my own mind, as though what I really wanted was written in her papers.

We go through this every time I call. She is wearing me down like an expert interrogator. I imagine Cordelia shaking hands with my father, looking like a compact car in her charcoal suit, my dad just thinking how to drive her off the lot. He chose this woman, this mortuary. What am I supposed to do now that his body has been delivered? It's no time for comparison shopping. I can't say, "I'm taking the body and leaving."

My brother and sister don't want to see the body, and I am not sure that I do either, but Jing Fei does, and since she has been assigned to me, that is my duty. Marshall takes the kids to his house to hang out with their cousins.

By now my brother has dug through enough of the paperwork to learn that Dad died $150,000 in debt to the federal government, not counting state taxes and HOA fees, and the house in Hawaii that we didn't know about, which is in foreclosure. Did he think he could run to the island when his troubles mainland caught up with him, or that Jing Fei would marry him when he presented the house in a last-ditch effort to persuade her, or could he even think like that anymore? Perhaps he only smelled plumeria and saw the spiky shadows of birds of paradise upon the walkway and did not know why.

His best friend, a cardiologist, has charitably invited us to have the memorial at his house, where half the hospital and all of his wives will gather on Sunday—his wives, who fought him tooth and nail over child support and alimony, will cry at his funeral. They will flirt with his fraternity brothers. His former patients will press my hands and tell me he was the wisest, kindest, best doctor they've ever known. Hippocrates said, "Medicine is of all the Arts the most noble," and I understand their need. My father fulfilled it well. Only, they didn't know him as a family man. In the garden the oldest of his grandchildren will play with the youngest during the service. My son will park the guests' cars wearing a baseball cap backward; my daughter will scoop ice cream to go with the pie. Later his poker buddies will remark in wonder at having never met any of his grandkids.

When Jing Fei finishes feeding the loner fish, we do our little hug-hug, and I force myself to tell her the bad news from the mortuary.

"I talked to the woman at Alameda Memorial Park this morning, and they won't let us see my father unless we pay for a full funereal viewing."

"Not worry," she says. "I call, speak to man this time. Say we need see your deddy dressed, for make sure everything good. Man, he say maybe, we come tomorrow afternoon."

"So, there's a man at the funeral home who will let us in?"

"Yes, I say we need taka your deddy nice clothes. I say I have pick him most comfortable shoes." She stops to take a nubby Kleenex out of her uniform pocket and dab her eyes. She points at a plastic bag by the door. "Your deddy say, these shoes most comfortable."

I nod gravely. "Thank you, Jing Fei, really, thank you."

"Welcome. Tomorrow afternoon, we talk softly, you know, and man take us see your deddy."

"What about Marshall?"

"Your brother Marshall say him no want to see your deddy."

"I know," I say. "Neither does Mazie. But we'll go."

"I tell him, your deddy, good man. You no listen when him dark face. He not right in head. He love you."

"Thank you, Jing Fei," I say, and then we look at the dining-room table, a stirred pile of bills, collection-agency notices, termination-of-service notices, check registers, and a Post-it pad that says, "Buy Port!" We take a deep breath at the same time. "He loved you," I say. She nods, swiping the tears across her cheeks with the palms of her hands. "You were good to him."

At three o'clock the next day, I drive my father's thirty-two-year-old diesel Mercedes Benz over to Qi-Li's Chinese Restaurant to pick up Jing Fei. We don't take her car, a Toyota Camry that my father gave her a few years ago. It is unspoken between us; the Benz was his war pony, so we drive it, drizzling oil across town. Over the years, my father spent a lot of cash to keep this car on the road—last of a dying breed, like himself.

On the dashboard of the Benz is a pink Post-it, and printed on it in block letters, as though he might not be able to make out his prescription-writing scrawl, is the word "Doughnuts!" In this alone I see his dark survival humor at work. So long as one can remember and locate doughnuts, life is still worth living. When I'd call on Sundays and ask him how he was, he'd answer, "Upright, mobile, and able to take nutrition." He didn't complain about his short-term memory loss or the weakness of his left arm.

I think about the number of times I tried to get my dad to see a different neurologist. When he hit his head in Hawaii, no one was able to tell us whether it was a stroke or not. Ten days on life support, and they ran every test on him. When my brother arrived at the hospital, his then girlfriend Rayona wouldn't get up off the couch where she was reading her magazine, though afterward she brought all the pills from the hotel medicine cabinet to the hospital.

My brother was the one who found the empty bottle of Viagra in the sock compartment of my father's suitcase. Viagra lowers blood pressure, and my father already had the blood pressure of a marathon runner, a trait that runs in the family. This low blood pressure blessing means I can't slam my feet to the floor in the mornings without giving myself a serious swoon. The doctors disagreed about the cause of his fall—one determined my father had had a stroke, the other insisted there were no signs of stroke. One thing was certain: my father had hit his head hard on a countertop going down. We kept quiet about the Viagra, and we sure as shit never discussed it with him. Maybe my father knew all along what was coming for his heart. He didn't want a new neurologist, and he wasn't about to give up his Viagra.

"Doughnuts!" My father's sign makes me feel I should stop and get us some on the way to the mortuary. The world puts a premium on the baker as well as the doctor. In a time of war these two might be spared, maybe even traded across enemy lines. In my father's cufflink box I find the blocky US pin that would have decorated his uniform as a doctor and captain, though he didn't put much store in rank. He was above all a man of character, and he was right that it is a word gone out of fashion. Forty years of medical practice, four wives, the girlfriends in between, the children, and he was only ever slightly eroded. The thought makes me teary.

This afternoon, Jing Fei has her mouth drawn on askew in plum lipstick and is wearing a black leather jacket over her nurse's aide pants. The jacket is Italian, a gift from my father I bet. Her eyes water at the edges, and she looks windblown by distress. She asks me where his clothes are, and after nodding at the back seat where I have laid them, she says nothing.

The undertaker introduces himself as Felipe Estrada and takes the clothes from our hands. He's a solid guy in a dark suit who walks like a big cat, all rolling motion. Jing Fei nods her head in little jerks at everything he says. She is dabbing at her eyes with a Kleenex so wadded it looks like popcorn. We are told to wait while they dress him. I try not to picture my father dead, naked, pushed into his clothes by other people's hands.

As we wait in the mortuary foyer, Jing Fei tells me about one time in Hawaii when my father's left arm shook real bad and he felt weak. "We going to go to doctor, but he feel betta. Your faddah. He stubborn man." I think back to my attempts to get him to get a second opinion from a neurologist. He could play a Shakespearean King, Sir Lawrence Olivier, for at least fifteen minutes, twenty maximum, and he'd chosen his court well—his young doctors were cowed by him. The only betrayer among them was his body.

"You may come in for the viewing now."

Few men own a tuxedo anymore, and I'm glad to see that my father would still make a handsome daguerreotype. His lips are turned up ever so slightly; it's his napping smile, the one he wore when he dozed on my brother's boat, safely away from his practice and his quarreling wives. We, his full-blooded children, protected him as though we might be able to keep him in our own Swiss Family Robinson, our own Shangri-La.

"He look just lika sleeping."

Jing Fei is running her hands down his body, her fingers rippling over his red silk vest, light as fingers trilling a piano.

"Looka good," she says. "Good thing he cut his hair, you know? He call and tell me he cut his hair."

My father's face is ruddy, as though he had been out sailing the day before.

Undertaker Estrada nods in my direction. "We often see this florid complexion in those who have suffered from an atherosclerotic cardiovascular event."

Does he think using these death certificate words will help any? Jing Fei does not even look up from her search for my father's socks and underwear. They have covered him up in a deep burgundy brocade. She scrabbles first at his feet to uncover the shiny black loafers we chose. Estrada stands back, arms folded like a museum guard. Together, our hands flicker up the side to uncover the black satin stripe along his pant leg, the red silk cummerbund at his waist. We have buried him in his best—my father, the fatherless scholarship boy whose family ran a laundry. For them, for him, we have buried him in a tuxedo. I rest my hands for a moment on my father's chest, then draw them back. His chest feels drawn up into a ridge. He is bird chested.

Estrada seems relieved that I have taken my hands off the body. "Your father was very strong for a man of his age."

"Yes," Jing Fei says nodding and smiling at him suddenly, "he very strong, lika man much younger." Then she turns abruptly toward my father. "Why you leave me here alone? Wendie. I want you come back. Why you leave me?" She shakes her wadded up Kleenex at him.

"I'll leave you for a few moments," says Estrada. The undertaker wends his whisper-quiet way out of the room, while Jing Fei has started a slow moaning that comes in constant waves—*unh, unh, unh.*

"I want you come back. I love you so much, Wendie. Only good man I found, you and my faddah. Only good man."

I am standing with my hands pressed to my mouth, immobilized by her display of feeling. Jing Fei bows and takes a sudden step back so that she is parallel with me. She shakes my arm. "You say now, to your faddah."

I look at her smeared face and feel her loneliness in this country of single-family dwellers. Dad's condo complex is built like a hamster habitrail where you only meet your neighbors when taking out the trash. Jing Fei came every week with a sack of fresh vegetables.

"You say him now." She nods at me, still dabbing and dabbing with the ruined Kleenex.

I step forward to look my father in the face. There's a scrape on his cheekbone, but it's not so bad, nor the one above his eye either. Jing Fei has returned to the slow moaning in waves—*unh, unh, unh*. I stroke my father's head; the short prickles are soft in my palm. I have never touched the top of his head before.

"Papa," I whisper, "I wanted you to see Norman. He's almost grown now, a young man. I wanted you to see Noelle. She is winning awards. I don't know why you couldn't love Mazie better. I don't know why you had to be so hard on Marshall. But we love you, Daddy, and we're all going to be together, Daddy, to say good-bye to you."

In my mind's eye, I see Marshall's sons and Mazie's daughter and my kids playing around the pool, the older ones holding a ball above the heads of the younger ones, then making a splashing shot that even the youngest can retrieve. I realize that in all the pairings my father made with women after our mother, the ages of the children stayed the same. The women grew younger as he grew older so their children would stay the ages we were when he left us. He always liked to explain music to me, the way a motif in a symphony was introduced, played in different keys, altered, then repeated in the coda. I see us now in every family he ever adopted, as an echo across time. Out of his reverberated, ricocheted love comes a terrible music. He asked me once to be the executor of his estate, but I refused to do his bidding without even knowing what it was.

"How could you think we would cut Mazie out of your will?" I nearly shout. "You left us nothing anyway, nothing but a pile of old computers and crockpots and never-opened telescopes. It's the principle of the thing, Dad. Isn't that what you used to say?"

I have taken his face into my hands, and I am slapping his jaw from side to side when Jing Fei grasps my wrists firmly and holds my hands up for us to see, like stiff chicken's feet. When she lowers them, she presses them together.

"In China, we do like this," and she bows with her hands pressed before her, once, twice, again, each time taking a step back from my father.

"You open the door for me, Wendie," she says. "You good man. Hit in the head. You no mean bad thing. You good man. Help many people."

As I bow behind Jing Fei, I bow to the good man, not the one created by my nurtured hurts and long grievances. I bow, understanding for the first time that no matter what messed-up things I do in my lifetime, no matter whose feelings I hurt in the long hurdle toward perceived happiness, what will count is the practice of good I undertook everyday, the small hope I carried into each exchange, the desire somewhere, in all of my failings, to have proved useful.

TOTALED

| | | | | | | | | | | | | | | | | | | | | | | | | | | | | | | | |

"Norman," I say into the voicemail of my son's phone, "if you don't answer pretty soon, I'm going to stop paying for this phone."

One minute later, it rings.

"Mom," he says. "I'm here, okay?"

"Yeah, but you're not *here*."

"We're about to jam. I'll be home later."

I hear various guitar twangings and reverb in the background.

"What time is later?" I have to shout.

"Mom, you act like I don't lay it down for you, but I do. I waited a fucking half hour for you and missed Shane's birthday dinner."

"You didn't tell me that."

"Gotta jam, Mom."

With that, I am left holding the red flip phone that reminds me of nothing so much as a raisin box.

My son's help around the house isn't part of some parenting program to ingrain good habits. Each week, I need him to carry the groceries, the firewood, and the laundry. If I lift too much, my insides inflame. The autoimmune disease I have is supposed to inflame my intestines. That I'm used to, but this year my disease decided to go on a road trip—first it went on a visit to my rib cage and inflamed my ligaments (I had an EKG so the doc could eliminate the possibility of angina), then to the muscles of my eyes (I had an MRI to eliminate the possibility of a brain tumor). Now that I've had my fake brain tumor and my fake heart attack, I figure I have a ten-year warranty on my body. I'm feeling I can handle anything, then last night my son splits for his friend's house without mowing the lawn or unloading the groceries after we have a screaming match over the chores. "You ask way too much of me!" he yells out the car window.

I spend the day on painkillers and dare to enter his room. The carpet appears to be growing chin hairs, there is so much loose tobacco scattered around. I find beer cans in the bathroom drawers and blueberries smashed under the couch cushions. Stoners. My position on marijuana has been compromised by the fact that I have on occasion asked my son for pot. I plead pain relief. When my bladder inflames, it feels like someone is grinding glass in there. Now my son offers pot to me all the time, as though it might replace the need to vacuum or take out the trash.

Don't get me wrong. I have asked my doctors for a prescription. The young urologist looked like he wanted to flee the room. The good-humored gastroenterologist told me there was no need for that and offered to put me on Humira, which can damage the liver and cause lymphoma. In the words of my GP, it's "the chemotherapy" of autoimmune diseases. My GP told me he'd write me a marijuana scrip and back me all the way to court, but since our local dispensary got shut down by the sheriff's office, I'm only making sure I can get my son out of jail if he gets pulled over. The phone rings again, and I find the raisin box under the newspaper.

"Mom," Norman says, "we've got to stop whompin' on each other. We're taking each other to the mat every time."

"Yeah, we've got to stop. I need to reserve my strength for going to work. I can't be chewing on you about the chores."

"You went off on me for not being there when you were late."

"I can't help it if the marketing takes me longer, Norman. Try to leave me more of a buffer next time. You're in and out of here so fast, all I see is a blur."

"Well, text me from the market next time, and I'll be there to bring the bags up."

"Norman?"

"Yeah?"

"Don't call me an impossible bitch. I may be in pain, but I am not an impossible bitch."

"It's not a big deal, Mom. It's like when one of my friends says, 'That's so gay,' and they don't mean homo. Or, 'Get over here, you ho.'"

"It's not casual to me. Your father used to say it when we fought."

"Okay, Mom. We're not going there. You can put down the razor."

"When will you be home? I left the dog food and the other heavy stuff in the car."

"I'm going to hang with the guys for a while."

"When you will be home?"

"*Mom*," he says with exaggerated patience.

"*Norman*," I say in the same tone.

"Mom," he says, and rings off.

My seventeen-year-old son is like some free-growing sprout; he has all the sweetness of wild licorice, but he's weedy and scraggly and determined to pry the pavers apart.

At 1:00 a.m. the phone rings. I have been dreaming one of those M. C. Escher dreams, except the architecture is rhetorical. I'm applying for disability, trapped inside a government phone system, punching the different options, but I keep getting the voice that tells me I have to prove I've been dead full-time.

"Hello?"

"Mom?"

There's hurt in his tone, and I snap to consciousness. "Norman. What is it?"

"Mom, my car is in a ditch."

"Where are you?"

"I went off Lakemont Boulevard."

"My God. Are you okay?"

"Yeah, Mom. I can walk home if you want."

"No, I'm coming to get you."

He is almost home, only a couple miles. I zip myself into a fleece robe and take a flashlight. As I crest the hill, the space between the trees opens like a channel of water. On the blackest stretch of road stands my son holding his lighter, flicking the flame with his thumb, the sudden strobe on his face sparking a trace image of him—my six-year-old boy who held his sparkler with both hands in front of him. We hug like drunk men on a heaving sea, weaving to keep balance.

"I'm not wasted, Mom," he says when I let go. "I'm not even stoned."

I search his face in the half-light. "I'm just glad you're in one piece."

I shine my flashlight off the side of the road. Thirty feet down the embankment his 1983 Mercedes is tipped sideways, its trajectory stopped by two huge fir trees. There's a glacial erratic the size of a dumpster beneath the car. The chassis slumps over the rock.

"Norman," I say, "you're lucky to be alive."

"I know," he says. "The Benz saved me."

I let my flashlight play over the wreckage. A block of the cement barricade has toppled and several boulders are overturned. The body of the car is tipped nearly vertical.

"How did you get out?"

"I pulled myself up by my armpits, I guess."

"It must have made a god-awful racket, grinding over all that stuff."

"Not really, Mom. I had the music up pretty loud."

I shine the flashlight up into his face. He's laughing, and I punch him in the arm. "Get in the goddamn car."

By the time I pull into the driveway, his mood has sobered. He takes my hand off the emergency brake and clasps it. "Really, Mom, thanks for coming to get me."

After I drop my son off at Bellevue College the next morning, I head to the local Fred Meyer's to pick up my prescriptions and enough bagels and cereal to keep Norman and Noelle fueled. At the checkout I head to my favorite gal, Connie, a woman my age with a swoop nose, Irish freckles, and three boys to call her own.

"You don't look so good, hon," she says.

"My son totaled his car last night."

"Is he all right?"

"Yes, thank God. Bent the frame and the floorboard, but some trees stopped him from going over."

"Sheez. Why is it these guys have to total a car before they pay attention? My oldest totaled two trucks. My youngest only one."

"I guess we got that out of the way."

"You sure did, honey. The trick is for 'em to total the car without getting hurt or hurting anyone else."

"Well, we got him a big old heavy Mercedes Benz, bought it like you would a bicycle helmet."

"Ain't that the truth? Did you get the car hauled out before the cops came?"

"No, should I?"

"Yeah, that way it won't go on his record and up his insurance rates. If the cops haven't found the car, you should get on it."

"Thanks, Connie. I guess I'm not thinking."

"No biggie."

"You sure are looking skinny," I say. "Those boys of yours giving you a hard time?"

"Nah, I got a new boyfriend."

"Oooh!" I sustain the exclamation, make it ride up and over a significant hill.

"You betcha." She's got a rhythm going between the scanner and register. "Today, he texts me, 'Nylons.'"

I nod enthusiastically and try not to look confused.

"He's taking me out. 'What shall I wear?' I says. He says, 'little black dress.'"

"Nice," I say, smiling. "You deserve happiness."

"Oh yeah," she says, motioning with the back of her hand to the keypad where I slide my card. "This one's a keeper. He already moved in with me."

On the way out to the car, I marvel at how fast some people my age can make the monumental decisions when it seems most of us are talking ourselves out of them, the whole claptrap of getting under one roof. I was swift in my twenties, slept with some young buck, did his laundry, moved in three days later, then spent four years extricating myself—I put so much energy into convincing myself I'd been in love with him in the first place. But now, with the end in sight, it seems to me that if you know you love someone, if you even think you know, why waste any time? Bully for you, Connie.

On my bad days I wonder if anyone would sign up to be with me. I'm still proud of my career, though I'm deflated by dinner and near dead by Fridays. I spend weekends in bed so I can get up and do it again, amen. Slater, Steiny & Alesandro has made me supervisor of the junior paralegals and legal secretaries. I'm the only one of my girlhood friends who has gone so far and gotten so sick. No, I have to amend that: One woman I know has died of cancer. And Tamara is gone. I've been knocked back but not knocked off. There's that, and it's almost everything.

By 11:00 a.m. I am again standing by the side of Lakemont Boulevard at the hairpin turn where Norman went into an unstoppable slide. The sky is delivering a steady pour, which I can hear fall as a wet percussion from branch to leaf. The yellow maple leaves on the black pavement give it a sudden three-dimensional depth. I'm waiting for Norman's father and the tow truck to appear. I can't tell which of the five medications I take every morning is coming on, but whether I tilt my head up toward the converging tree tips or down toward the deepening pavement, I feel that the back of my head is floating and I should make swimming motions to ensure it stays that way.

This morning, when I told Guy that Norman damn near died last night, he pooh-poohed me. Guy had wanted Norman to have a Japanese car because it would get better mileage than two tons of German steel. But our son's driving style is "romp and stomp," and I would have none of it. I taught Norman to drive in the graveyard because, as I told him, "everyone here is already dead." This morning Guy said, "Big heavy car like that, you can't right it once it goes into a slide." He sucked air through his teeth, waiting for the impossible bitch to take the bait, but I didn't say a darn thing. I won't fight anymore. These days I conserve my energy.

When I was married I tried to be living proof that women can have it all, and I busted my health doing it. In America it seems you're either overworked or your work life is over. As I clawed my way to paralegal, I met wives who were once lawyers and doctors who had opted out of the marketplace to stay home full-time. They were the ones most attached to attachment parenting. I say if the kid can unbutton your blouse, nursing is over, but these highly educated moms have to believe their presence is an absolute necessity. I get that, but have they read the Gallup Polls? Stay-at-home moms are the most depressed.

In theory my husband was all about women's rights and equity in the domestic realm, which means he talked a good game right up until the babies arrived, and then it became apparent that Guy still regarded me as the caretaker and himself as the provider. Hard to shake for the both of us. I still regarded myself as the caretaker. I'd go to market at ten o'clock at night, after the kids were in bed and after I'd answered the late-day email. To his credit, Guy would come out when I got home and haul in the grocery freight. Then he'd shut off the TV and go to bed. I'd stay up and read legal briefs. Our fantasies then were of sleep, of luxurious beds in hotel rooms with nobody in them.

In the garage I have a file of all the recriminatory emails we sent to each other after we separated. I put it in a folder with kittens on the front and wrote BURN on the inside, but I haven't done it yet. Why do I keep a record of such pain? He told me once I was like a bomb whose fuse he had to keep stomping out. But to me he was like a mail-order prize you win only to find in small print "not redeemable for six months to a year subject to the following conditions."

Perhaps I keep the file because love is the greatest puzzlement of all. How can you sum up fifteen years of championing each other's causes, of folding each other's families into the preexisting craziness of your own, of believing wrongly that you had something between you that could outlast the marriages of friends crumbling all around you? How could you total it? In the end we were our own episode of ER, both of us trying to shock the patient back to life, applying the paddles while turning the voltage higher and higher. To no avail. But *the trying* should count for something. It should, but there's nowhere to make a record of it. When I tell people I'm divorced, I always add, "We had a good run. Fifteen years."

Guy pulls up in his little Japanese car and gives me a clipped hello. He always wears a worried Papa Bear expression, like he's waiting for the oatmeal to cool—just the right amount of stern mixed with the right amount of protection—except around me, he looks perpetually alarmed, like I'm going to serve up a big spoonful of something scalding.

This morning he's all business, reconstructing the accident from the evidence.

"You can see where he fishtailed," he says, using his arm for a pointer. "His wheels locked up here . . ." Guy's voice dwindles as his eyes travel over the brink and slide down the steep. "Look at that," he says.

"Yes," I say. "It's shocking."

"He broke the cement barricade," Guy says, needing to narrate it for himself.

"And mowed down those trees," I say, taking my turn to point.

"Christ, he tore up that boulder, and if it hadn't of been for those—"

We stare at the pale blue Mercedes propped sideways against the thick Douglas fir. As I stand beside him I feel his lean, tamped-down energy, my own effusive plumpness, but I am determined not to complete his sentences for him. We stare and stare together.

"Maeve," he says at last, "you were right to insist on that big heavy car."

He turns his wound-weary face toward me as an offering of love, and we throw our arms around each other, hugging in a gesture that echoes the staggering embrace of the night before, all blame retreating from the kingdom our marriage once made— before us the darkness of the death bird flapping and flapping, retreating finally beyond the trees.

SELF-DEFENSE

||||||||||||||||||||||||||||||||

I locate our self-defense class not because the sign is big, but because it is so wide; it juts off the building like a protest placard. The sign is wide in order to fit the words "Effective Results Training & Mixed Martial Arts," and below it specifies "Brazilian, Jiu Jitsu, Kenpo Karate, Muay Thai Kickboxing," and "Self-Defense," in case we missed the point. Inside the dojo we take our seats on a wooden bench in the narrow foyer, which faces the office window. The blinds are not drawn, so my daughter and I watch as a boy of twelve or thirteen, wearing his *gi*, comes in with his mother and flops down in the one chair across from the desk. Sensei Lucas stands; he is at least half as wide as the desk itself. He motions toward the boy's mother, who is still standing. He glares at the boy and juts his thumb in the air. The boy leaps out of his chair and offers it to his mother with exaggerated chivalry. The muscles of Lucas's forearms rotate and flex as he plants his hands on the desk and leans out over them, resembling nothing so much as a large gold toad.

I turn away and read a homily affixed to the wall in a small black frame: "I came into this world kicking and screaming while covered in someone else's blood, and I have no problem with going out the same way."

I exhale emphatically, and next to me Noelle snorts because she finds my involuntary noises irritating. I have learned over time that my very breathing is annoying.

I shift my eyes to the wall space on the other side of the office window. I can't help but notice that Lucas is standing now, lightly tapping his fingertips against the drum of his belly. The mother cranes her head to look up at him.

Behind her head is a cross stitch, Psalm 144:1, and I can just make out the words "Blessed be the Lord my rock, who trains my hands for war, and my fingers to fight." I consider the rock that David put in his slingshot to slay Goliath. Perhaps the Lord is that rock.

Lucas rounds the corner into the foyer, all raspy bluster, "Come on now, ladies. Let's do this thing." We follow him obediently into the mirrored room and sit down on mats in a semi-circle. He remains standing, a gold Aztec toad god.

"Girls, I don't have to tell your mothers this because they already know it, but I am gonna tell you. Ninety percent of adult rape victims are women. That's right, one out of every six women is the victim of an attempted or completed rape in her lifetime." He slaps the fingers of one hand into the palm of the other so that it comes out "in"—*slap*—"her"—*slap*—"lifetime"—*slap*. Noelle is fixed on his every word even though she didn't want to come to this workshop an hour ago. When she feels me staring at her, she turns her head and hisses, "What?" So much for that old saw about needing a common enemy to be united.

"Mothers, you should feel good about yourselves because you're doing the right thing." *Mothers.* This is how he will address us bleary-Saturday-morning women for the rest of the class. I kind of like it: *Mothers.*

"Let me just start by saying, I am so glad you are here. I don't mean to scare you mothers and your daughters, but I am a former cop, and you are here because you know there's a problem. You know you gotta be tough, cuz you were taught to 'be nice,' you know, 'Be nice and pass the candy bowl.'

"Not in here. In here, fighting is your mind-set. General George Patton said, 'A good plan violently executed now is better than a perfect plan executed next week.'"

Lucas then shows us a film clip. It's the scene in *Braveheart* where King Edward throws his son's lover out of the castle window.

"Cool scene, right?" He doesn't wait for anyone to answer, and with our necks craned, we look like eaglets ready to be fed with an eyedropper.

"The king wasn't young; he wasn't stronger. He was wily. He got the guy to walk to the window by pretending he wanted to show off the castle grounds. He put his hand on the guy's back, all fatherly, and then boom, he shoves him off balance in one swift move. Yes, good old King Edward employed some leverage techniques, but first," and here Lucas taps against his temple with his index finger, "he used his noggin, that's right, ladies, the old think tank above the shoulders." Lucas moves toward us, takes a squat stance, looks around like he's scanning for danger. I think he's corny as hell, but the teenage girls are watching his every move, so what do I care?

"Ladies, if you're in a sketchy situation, you get that spidery feeling, listen to it. If you have to, use manipulation to outsmart the guy. Whatever you do, don't do nothing."

"Remember, to live, you got to win, and I don't mean win like you would at checkers, I mean remember *What's Important Now*. Got it? An acronym. You panic, you're jammed up. And your body won't go where your mind hasn't. That's why we're here." I can hear the woman next to me breathing. It sounds like she is counting beats to her breathing—inhale 1–2–3–4, exhale 1–2–3–4. She turns to me and offers a winsome smile. Lucas doesn't seem to draw breath.

"Say you're in this situation, the guy has got a gun to your back and says, 'Walk with me.' What should you do? Freeze and submit? No, you want to sound like you're on his side. Say, 'Hey dude, there's a camera, you better get out of here,' or, 'Hey dude, they're calling the cops.'"

Noelle is scanning the room, her neck taut.

"You know anyone?" I whisper.

"Shush. No."

Her shoulders lower. She is relieved not to know anyone.

I asked Noelle's fourth-grade teacher not to make Noelle eat at the head of the table in the lunchroom—we would accept the risk of peanut butter between bread—and I asked why she thought it was that Noelle still complained of being excluded.

"Well, it's just that she is really creative and has a big vocabulary. She uses words the other kids don't know."

I hadn't considered the need to dumb Noelle down. Then in February her teacher called to let me know that the kids had asked if they could write, "You're weird," on Noelle's Valentines. The teacher used a high-pitched singsong voice. "So, I asked the kids, do you mean 'weird' in a good way or a bad way?" She had allowed it. She hoped I didn't mind.

I wish I'd had my "What the fuck?" ready that day. I wish I'd asked if she'd tried substituting "bizarre," "freakish," or "strange" for "weird" before giving permission. I am a slow reactor sometimes. In March a new girl came and sat next to my girl. They became peas in a pod; they laughed at their own jokes all day. But in May a new order asserted itself. Amy, whose family spent spring break in Cabo, came back with a gold anklet and friendship rings for her circle on the playground.

"One for you, and one for you, and oops. I don't have one for you. I guess I ran out . . ."

Amy said this to Noelle while wearing a friendship ring on her own hand.

Lucas shows us a short, greenish, grainy video of a bunch of people standing in line at a mini-mart. As the video starts, Noelle moves across the room from me. I notice that the other mothers and daughters are still sitting side by side, and I suffer a small stabbing sensation in my chest, as though someone were using one of those ornamental samurai swords that tourists buy in Japan. Back in the mini-mart, there's no volume and a hulk of a man takes offense because somebody bumped him or stepped on his toe. He lifts his arms, head jutting forward, clearly shouting at the guy in front of him, who hunches inside his hoody. The other people in line draw away. Out of nowhere Hulk gob-smacks Hoody then follows it with a blow to the head. Hoody goes down, and Hulk gets in a few kicks. The crowd splits into a semicircle around the fallen. You can't hear the gasping, but you know it's there. Hulk exits hard, and his girlfriend gets the blast wave as the door swings back at her, but she shoves it and follows him out.

"So, was anybody there in a fighting mind-set besides the aggressive guy?"

"Not really," says a tall wraith of a girl. "I was kinda surprised . . ." Her voice trails off at the end like air escaping a balloon. She twists one tennis shoe on its toe.

"Why didn't anyone help him?" asks a mother in siren-green Adidas leggings. She's holding a Starbucks coffee, and I wish she would share it with me.

"Egg-zactly," says Lucas. "And here's the thing: they outnumbered him. They are just standing around waiting for someone else to do the saving. We always think someone else will save us. The natural-born warrior is weaned out of us."

I look across at Noelle. Her hair is pulled up in a high ponytail, and I imagine the fine hairs at the back of her neck. I used to be able to kiss her there as many times as I wanted, and she smelled delicious to me, like the sunny vanilla of a ponderosa pine. Last night she fell asleep with her phone in her hand. I went in to pull the covers over her. Here's what I read, what I think I read:

> If you so much as talk
> to Chuck at hoco
> I will bash yr face in.
>
> > I don't even want to
> > talk to him.
>
> You lie.
>
> > Ask Marsha.
>
> Whateevuuurrr.

"Who eats meat here?" Lucas bellows. Hands shoot up. "So, you rip flesh every day. Not a big deal. Ears also tear real easy. Bones break way easier than you think. Snap a finger, stomp on their feet. Ribs break real easy. You puncture the lung and shut 'em down. Remember, you are the weapon." Noelle gives me a significant look that I don't know how to interpret, and I wonder how it is possible to live with someone who utterly mystifies you.

It's not that I haven't read the articles about cyberbullying and about the children who've killed themselves. I have. The newspaper said the mother did everything right, except *this*, except *something* . . . I don't remember. The mother contacted the school then lodged a formal complaint, then she shut down her daughter's Facebook page, monitored her daughter's phone, and transferred her to a new school. Then the article went on to fault the mother. I don't remember which mother. There have been so many. Maybe she couldn't do everything right. How many of us can? If I tell Noelle to give me her phone, she says, "You can't take my phone away. Dad gave it to me, and he pays for it."

If I take it away anyway, he texts me, "Give Noelle her phone back. I need to be able to contact her." Or she decamps to his house. I have no access to Noelle's Facebook page either. Her father set it up, and he says it should be her choice. Noelle says she doesn't trust me. I hear about her FB page from my mother or my neighbor. Allegiances, alliances, favoritism. Is this how humans have always formed separate bands? Last week Noelle paid a surprise visit, calling from the kitchen, "I knew you'd have better food than Dad." It's in the little things. I too have wanted to go down in history as the better parent. I too seek most-favored-nation status despite my claims of neutrality.

I bring my focus back to Lucas, and I try to decide why he looks so much like a gold toad. He lacks a neck in front; instead there's this pouch of skin that sways beneath his broad chin and undulates in folds to settle against his chest. He points a finger at me as though I were agreeing with him, and I nod vigorously.

"We use knives every day, in the kitchen. You see a creepy-looking guy holding a knife, it's him you're scared of. So who is our idol here? You are, ladies. You are your own IDOL. And that's another one of my little handy acronyms. *IDOL* stands for *In Defense of Life.*"

I have an urge to raise my hand. I want to ask, "What about soul death? What about violation of the psyche? What about mob rule once removed?"

At the new elementary school Noelle attended after the divorce, the students played recorders, and the library had skylights. The available parcel of land for the new school put it in the hills above the lake, where there was no view, and those who lived in the big, skylighted houses that looked like the library would drive up the hills to drop off their kids near the trailer parks with the tarped roofs and the women's shelter back in the woods. We lived in the town's first affordable housing—townhouses that had been put up in three days and that now seemed to lean on each other rather than share common walls.

Instead of cake or cookies, parents were supposed to bring a book to be read on the birthday child's day, then donated to the library. Christie's mother must not have read the memo. Mrs. Karlsson brought a big box of store-bought cupcakes in her brown Bronco, which she double-parked out front in the bus zone. Noelle told me that Mrs. Karlsson came from the women's shelter every week to eat lunch with Christie because Christie was in foster care and Mrs. Karlsson hadn't got her back from the courts yet. The teacher turned away the frothy, rainbow-specked cupcakes that Christie's mother held in her arms, turned the woman away, and Mrs. Karlsson marched the cupcakes back out to the Bronco while the mothers volunteering in the library peered through the oblong windows. "Mother," Noelle said, "I wouldn't have cared that I couldn't have a cupcake."

Lucas is amped; he swings his arms back and forth across his chest. "Now we are going to practice throwing punches. Thumb across, never inside." He shows us his fist: exhibit A. "What's the biggest misperception about throwing a punch?"

The girl in the washed-out T-shirt mumbles something. It's all Lucas needs to continue, and to his credit, he never tells the girls they are wrong. "That's right, you don't punch with the first set of knuckles. You punch with the ridge. And it comes at an angle, from the hips. Let your punch pivot."

I look down at my hand—big-boned for a woman. I remember my uncles teaching my brother to box, jabbing and feinting. I remember the babysitter who knew judo and flipped my brother over and onto his bed. I make a fist. Have I ever made a fist before?

If you so much as talk to Chuck at hoco I will bash yr face in.

Hoco . . . must mean homecoming. At breakfast Noelle was thumb-punching and checking her phone mid-spoonful, scowling into the screen.

"What's the flurry?" I asked.

"Okay, Mom. You really want to know?" She sets down her spoon, not the phone.

"Yes, I really want to know."

"There's this girl in the perfect crowd, and she thinks I am trying to steal her boyfriend."

"Do you think he likes you?"

"Yep. On Friday, when he shoved me in the hall, I body-slammed him. Get the message, dude."

"He might still think you're flirting."

"No way, Mom."

She does not fly under the radar, my girl, that's all I know. Then it was time to go to the martial arts studio for this self-defense class.

"So let's talk about bad advice," Lucas says, walking back and forth while softly smacking a fist into his other hand. "Lotta people gonna tell you that if you just give in, you'll survive. Who knows that, ladies? Who knows that, mothers? Ted Bundy was real charming, and he killed every one of them. Say the worst thing happens. You're fighting off this attacker, and he overpowers you. I say keep on fighting. Because the more DNA of his you leave around you, the more likely this criminal is to get caught."

I've never thought of this; I wonder how you could think about the crime scene you're leaving behind while fighting for your life?

"Say a guy bear-hugs you from behind. Chances are he's bigger than you. You can't throw him off.

"Say he gets something around your neck." Lucas motions to his assistant Duncan, who is flexing a canvas belt in his hands. Duncan is wearing chest pads but would probably look like a Teletubby even without them; he is rotund, affable, sweet-faced—and three hundred pounds. "You should have heard the guy coming, but maybe you had your earbuds in or you were texting on your phone, awareness down. That's a mistake, ladies. Not the warrior mind-set. Okay, so you're walking, and he comes up from behind with his belt."

Lucas walks, hums, and pretends to punch buttons on an imaginary phone. Duncan comes up from behind him and loops the belt around his neck. "You only got seconds now, ladies, because he's got your carotid arteries under pressure, the big ones on either side of your neck, and you're going to pass out in a few seconds. Your natural urge is to hunch and pull away. That only makes the band tighter and gives him more leverage. You gotta do the opposite, you gotta turn sideways, free one side of the neck, and lunge toward him, strike his face, smack his ear. Remember his hands are on either side of the belt.

"Let's try that. Who's going to demo with me?"

Noelle is rocking up on the balls of her toes. Her ponytail swishes as she looks to the right and left, to see who will step forward. A tall, manicured girl in a t-back sports bra and matching leggings steps up. Noelle crosses her arms.

Imperious doesn't describe Noelle's demeanor some days—she is not merely a queen, this fourteen-year-old daughter who once loved me, she is a queen giving a performance, offering a public viewing to her thousand minions. I am, unfortunately, one of the dimmer and more doltish of her subjects. Last night Noelle and I cleaned my closet.

"This hippy-wear has got to go," she said, slapping back the hangers in my closet as she reviewed my wardrobe. My ankle-length skirts were falling to the floor. "I'm glad I made you buy a black pencil skirt," she said, eyeballing it with approval.

"I did get compliments that day."

"Of course you did. You looked hot."

She wrenched on more hangers to part the sea of clothes and identified a new offender.

"You may not touch that," I said. "It has sentimental value. I used to wear it to concerts."

She looked at my velvet patchwork coat and sniffed. My grandmother used to say the word "piffle" and walk away. It was not so long ago that Noelle used to wheedle her way into bed with me for cuddles and chats. I miss seeing her face six inches from mine. Now she snatches her arm away when I touch her.

She snick-snacked through a few more hangers.

"Whatever you do, get rid of this bathrobe."

"But Regina gave me that," I protested.

"God, Mother, don't you remember the last time you wore it? I could have died right then and been happy."

I did remember. It was the fall after my father died and Noelle had started high school. She had forgotten the check I'd written for school lunch on the kitchen table. When I saw it there I knew she'd have to skip lunch, go hungry. So I threw on a coat without buttoning it and jumped into the 1986 Mercedes-Benz diesel my father had left behind after sinking three thousand dollars into the transmission and even more on preliminary bodywork. I guess he was planning to repaint his warhorse. Big burred-out whorls on the hood and roof where the paint had been taken down to the metal looked like gray crop circles. It was what I had to drive after the soccer-mom van crapped out on me, and I was grateful to have it.

That morning, I cinched my purple-paisley robe around my waist and flew out the door. Happy to see the line of children still at the bus stop, I slowed to look for Noelle.

"You forgot your lunch money," I called, holding the check out the window where it flapped.

As she stepped forward we heard the rumble of the bus engine behind us, and she gave me the last sweet smile of girlhood, though I did not know it then. I pulled forward quickly and made a U-turn that ended beside the stop sign. A quick head check and I lumbered home, congratulating myself on having caught her.

She came in that afternoon and scolded me.

"Mom, you drove up in your pajamas."

"No I didn't. I had a coat on over."

"Well, the kids could see your purple bathrobe."

"Oh, big deal."

"It is a big deal. They said, 'How come your mom drives a beater?' They called your car a hooptie."

"Honestly, it's a Mercedes-Benz. I mean, I know it needs bodywork."

"No, Mom. You don't get it. The bus driver said to me when I got on, 'Is that woman in the purple pajamas your mother? Well, you tell her she just ran a stop, and next time I'll have to report her.'"

"She said that in front of all the kids?"

"Yep, Mom, she did."

"That's shaming. If she has something to say to me, she should—"

"Just never mind, Mom."

"I'm going to call and let that woman know—"

"Just drop it, Mom, please."

After that, when I offered to pick her up from school, she told me no. If I came for a school event, I made sure to park in the lower lot, as per her instructions. Once, dropping off a doctor's note, I stood in the atrium of the school as the lunch bell rang, five hundred youths thundering down the two feeder stairways, seeking their groups, reconfiguring out of commotion. "It's like roving packs of wild dogs, Mom," Noelle said to me that night. And the child smile was replaced with new expressions I didn't recognize, ones she tried on every morning in the mirror, like outfits, fixed to match as she prepared for auditions that took place each day.

Last night the purple-paisley bathrobe wound up in the Salvation Army pile, both of us relieved to see it go. The warhorse was finally gone, sold and replaced with a Nissan Cube I leased recently, now respectably parked in the studio lot.

"You see that, ladies?" Lucas says. "Brittany just delivered a powerful ear clap. Good for you, Brittany, you done your ma proud. An ear clap drives an extra surge of air pressure into the ear canal and can rupture an eardrum. Way to go.

"Questions, mothers? Ladies?"

"What if a man puts you in a headlock from behind?" asks a girl with a teased-up hive, thick eyeliner, and a brass nose ring that makes the side of her nose a little greenish when you get up close. "My brothers used to do that." She laughs freely.

"Then you must know. What do you do?"

"Scream for Mom?" She laughs again, and the other teenagers laugh with her. "Kick 'em in the shins?"

"You could stomp on his feet," the girl's mother gamely offers. She's heavyset with the grainy skin of a long-term smoker, in stretch jeans and a Go Mariners sweatshirt.

"Heck yeah," Lucas says. "Doesn't matter where you stomp— toe, instep, ankle—it's all good.

"The Green River Killer, he strangled his victims from behind, forty-nine of them." Lucas snaps his fingers "What else are you going to do? You've got seconds to react."

"You could hammer-fist him in the groin," Noelle says, her feet planted, her eyes narrowed.

"Egg-cellent," Lucas says. "Smart girl we have here. You still have range of motion with one arm, limited, but enough to do some real damage. Plant the blow to a soft target, ladies."

A few giggles pass around the circle.

"Let's say you get around so now you're facing your attacker. Say the guy has got you by the shoulders and he's bringing you in close." Here Lucas has his baby-faced assistant stand in for the villain. "The guy grabs you by the shoulders. What can you get free? One arm." Duncan has stepped forward and grabbed Lucas by the shoulders. "Use it. Bring your elbow up like this, it's a club. It's an ancient trauma weapon. Wham to the jaw on the upstroke, then hammer-fist, and bash on the downstroke. Blunt force, ladies. Our aim is to do more than inflict pain. Our aim is to injure.

"Let's rehearse this. Let's go through the motions."

My partner is Abby, a neuro-sonographer. She is a mildly pretty highlighted blonde straight out of a commercial for a gated community on a golf course. Her jogging suit bears name brands. These are the kinds of nasty generic things American women think about each other every day. Her elbow strikes and hammer blows are tentative, her expression one of consternation, as though she were trying to learn a new Zumba routine.

"Hit harder, "I say. "Get into it."

She makes small grunts this time. Then it is my turn, and I try to imagine how she would describe me with my Stevie Nicks shaggy-but-on-purpose tousle and my debrided yet pilly fleece pullover—too old to be a rock'n'roll ingenue but too political to go suburban. I guess that's me.

"Hit it," Lucas yells, and I step in toward her, alternating arms and blows, which she meets adeptly with the vinyl baton. *Thud, whack, thud, whack.* With each impact, sounds crunch in my throat, emit as low grunts. Now it is her turn.

Abby's pupils are dilated—huge, dark pools of tar. I can't detect any expression there. "Hit it," Lucas yells. Her punches glance off the black vinyl vest. There's no force behind them—detached punching, if that's possible.

"Go ahead," I tell her. "Mess me up." She hunches down into her stance and dances on the balls of her feet. Her punches pop up a little more, but not much. "C'mon," I bark. "Fuck me up." *Slam, dance, slam.* Now her punches are connecting, her face—only a few feet from my own—is knotted at the center, her mouth and eyes pulled in toward her nose.

"You sick fuck," she says, but she is not looking at me, only at the point of impact each time. "You sick, sick fuck." Her punches are coming so hard and fast I don't have time to alternate my arms, and I bring my back leg up to stabilize my stance.

"Time," Lucas yells.

Abby has her hands on her cheeks, "Oh God oh God oh God, I hope I didn't hurt you."

"No," I say, "I get it. I'm fine." But is she fine? I don't think so. I think half the women in this room are having flashbacks.

As if he knows it, Lucas says, "Coffee break, ladies. Time to back it down."

Noelle and I head to the kiosk across the street where she orders a double-shot caramel macchiato and I have a café au lait. She doesn't seem to mind standing next to me out here.

"I'm sorry I was in a bad mood last night, Mom."

"Did something happen?"

"I was all right until I read this math problem about a group of friends baking cookies for a bake sale. The number of chocolate-chip cookies baked was four more than twice the number of oatmeal cookies made, blah, blah, blah, which made me realize I don't have any friends to bake cookies with."

I reach out and smooth a lock of her hair. She doesn't pull away. I make a sad face and put a finger under one eye. "It won't be like this when you get to college."

"It's cool, Mom," she says. "Let's go in."

Lucas calls my daughter Itty Bitty, as in, "Where's Itty Bitty?"

"Hey, Itty Bitty. Demo this with me. You know how to kick hard."

I wonder if I should find this nickname offensive. He calls her to demonstrate a knee-to-face blow—"See that, you draw his face right down into it." Then kick-cycling to get out of a trap.

"That Ted Bundy dude, he took the door handle off, but she didn't notice cuz he was such a gentlemen. So now how is she gonna escape? Only one thing to do: brace your back against that door and kick each leg like a piston."

During the demo my diminutive gymnast daughter delivers rapid-fire power strokes—ignition, explosion, propulsion—*bam,*

bam, bam. Her heels against his protective vest sound like a drum solo.

"Okay, I need another kicker. How about you, Noelle's mom? You look rough and ready."

Panic hits me as though dry ice were dropped in my lungs. "I don't know." I say. "I don't know."

Noelle is nodding. "C'mon, Mom, you can do it."

I used to be able to rely on myself. Now my body is like an air mattress with a pinhole leak. I can't just jump out into the middle of the lake without a care.

Lucas is talking, and Noelle is still nodding. He wants me to come at him with as many combinations as I can for sixty seconds. I take the center of the ring and come at him—elbow stroke, hammer fist, a direct punch to the chest that bounces me back on my ass. He's yelling, "Feet now, feet!" I piston-kick, I lunge for his ears. I hear cheering. Someone blows a whistle. I see all the faces I was bashing—Amy from fourth grade, Noelle's teacher, the teenager inside the phone . . . *This is idiotic*, I think. *Get a grip.*

Lucas is holding me at arm's length. Up close his eyes are light green, no, more than green, gold specked. "Are you all right?" he asks, and I nod. Then louder and more theatrically, he says, "Are we all good?" The women burst into clapping. Noelle rushes up and throws her arms low around my waist as though she were going to pick me up. "You rocked it, Mom. You're stronger than you think!"

Lucas says, "Okey dokey, then, who's next?"

Pretty soon the others take their turns, and I hear sounds I haven't heard since I labored to give birth, like the snarling vocalizations of Big Foot on the infamous Sierra tapes—whoops, growls, screams, guttural mumbles. Abby collides into me as she staggers out of the circle. She looks at me, breathing hard. Her pupils are still dilated. Words rush out of her mouth toward me.

"He pinned me when the exam door closed. Hollering out of his mind, 'I want a woman! I want a woman!' Finally, someone jumped on his back." She is wheezing into my face. "Two weeks later they want me to go back to work. They act like I'm faking an illness. I can't breathe in those tiny rooms. I can't breathe."

"You've been traumatized," I say, putting my hands on her shoulders. "What about taking medical leave?"

"They don't want me to take it," she says. "They want me to be just fine."

"Well, you're not, and you're going to have to insist on your own value. Because no one else is going to do it for you."

Noelle is watching us. She smiles at me. She puts her hands up like lion claws, the hands you would use to tell a scary story to a toddler. I don't understand for a moment. Then I see the space between them, in the shape of a heart.

THE WHORE OF HEALING

||||||||||||||||||||||||||||||

"Mom," my daughter says, "what age were you when you lost your virginity?"

Do I want to tell her? No. I was the same age as she is. I was just fourteen. Do I tell her? Yes.

"It was not a happy thing," I say. "I wouldn't wish it for you."

She wants to know everything then and there, but she doesn't get to.

A week later we fight because I won't let Noelle go to a new friend's house for an overnight. The parents aren't going to be home from work until four in the morning, and the eighteen-year-old brother will be in charge. It all sounds pretty sketchy, but I know Noelle is frantic for new friends since she was exiled from a quasi-popular pack over Christmas break.

"You need to get her mother's phone number," I say.

"Becky doesn't know it."

"She doesn't know her own mother's phone number?"

"Her mother got a new cell phone."

"Then the answer is no. If there is not an adult in the house, you don't stay the night. I can pick you up at ten."

"Mom," she says, sticking her chin out to let me know she is a badass hip-hop biotch, in case I don't know what I'm in for. "You are the only parent who cares about this kind of stuff. The other kids say to me, 'Oh, you have a parent like tha-at.' They feel sorry for me."

She's a foot from my left ear, and I'm making us oatmeal before work and school. "I guess that makes me the one parent with good judgment," I say.

"What do you think, Mom?!" she shouts at the side of my face. "That I'm going to act like some slut, like you?"

I snap the burner off in time to see her turn tail and light out for her room. She knows she's done it now. I shove the pan to the back of the stove. No one's hungry anymore.

After Noelle has left for school, I go to the garage to have a look at my old journals—whole composition books full of bad sex. I have to steel myself. It was a different era. How am I to convey that to my daughter, who already has no patience with me? She calls me an old hippie and tells me what clothes I should throw away. But I'm not an old hippie; I'm only a child who came of age in the wake that the sixties left behind.

I was twelve years old in 1972, the year the Supreme Court legalized birth control regardless of marital status. The doctor who put me on the pill when I was fourteen asked three questions: How old are you? (I lied.) How much do you weigh? (I lied.) Are you sexually active? (No, but I was not going lose my boyfriend, which was what the older girls assured me would happen.)

At fourteen I attended an alternative school on an island off the West Coast, a 1970s equivalent of the democratically run Summerhill School in England, except that drugs, sex, and absolute chaos forced its closure in less than two years.

As students of Salbatora Island School, we knew the canyons and coves with our feet, and slipped out of our dormitories like the lithe shadows we were when the evening dorm check had passed. Then we congregated in the canyons to revel, drinking tequila sunrises in tennis-ball cans. We kayaked to town on booze runs. We sailed to remote coves to enact our own version of Lina Wertmüller's *Swept Away*. The remoteness of the island untamed us all—if teenagers are ever really domesticated. When the rains came and washed out the roads, the faculty became lovers with their students, the students had shower parties in the dormitories, and wild boar roamed the halls.

On Salbatora Island we saw ourselves as a microcosm of utopia, a tribe of a small planet. At the school we didn't trust any governance but our own. The student body held town meetings in the library and locked the doors. No faculty allowed. I remember how a thief was dealt with. We sweated and breathed the air of swollen volumes while the dorms were searched by upperclassmen. A senior named Ryan ran the meeting and commanded guards to the French doors so that no one could leave. I thought Ryan looked like Bob Dylan because he had a frazzle of hair and a bent-inward look and seemed not to want the cowl of authority. The perpetrator confessed, broke down crying. Punishments and reparations were determined by student vote in front of him. I sat in my homemade wraparound skirt and halter top, inwardly quivering because I had never taken part in absolute rule. When we voted, the perpetrator was sent off island, with or without faculty consent.

The fragility of our society on the island was mirrored in the history—Indians, smugglers, gold miners, and traders who came before us, those specters who conceded to the dirt but not to rest. Never that. Islands are different that way, full of marooned ghosts; we were convinced of it.

The tectonic plates moved and our island with them. Salbatora had never been connected to the mainland. Claimed by the Spanish Empire, charted under the authority of the Viceroy of Mexico, the sea-otter trade flourished and resembled the extirpation of that other native population—the Indians. In the canyon at night we passed the ancient middens. Several students claimed they'd started choking when they entered the grove where the burial mounds lay, dark shell-circled hummocks.

"You could feel it, man, I'm not kidding, going for the throat, cutting off your air."

In the cold garage I sit on an ice chest and take the top off a cardboard file box. Stacked above my head are my children's drawings and rock collections and school photos in plastic bins on gunmetal-gray racks. When I crack the spine of the first journal, I smell both dampness and dryness, mildew and sage. The notebook begins with lyrics from "The Lee Shore" by Crosby, Stills, Nash, and Young transcribed in my own hand. The girl I was must have opened to the first page in the optimism of morning, because my letters don't look drunk yet the way they do on other pages, sprawling and slumping from margin to margin. I like to think the students shared a group innocence on that island, regardless of the alcohol and drugs, but perhaps that is nostalgia on my part.

October 12

I think I am in love with my brother's best friend, Tad. He keeps finding little reasons to touch me — he tucks my dress tag back in, or he compares my hair color with his by holding a lock of his next to mine so that our heads almost touch. He says only true Polacks like himself can have brown eyes with blonde hair. He's from Chicago, plays guitar. When I ask him why he plays "Needle and the Damage Done" so often, he says his brother came home from Vietnam a junkie.

Could've seen that one coming, Tad said and laughed, except it was this sad little laugh. He said his parents are raising his brother's child.

Guess they couldn't handle having a teenager and a toddler.

Does Tad like me? Marshall says he does.

October 14

Mom must think I am a paper doll, to be moved and marched many times. I didn't want to leave our last house. I'd actually planted some corn and tomatoes in the back. Now we live in Maddie's house, and nowhere in it feels like my space. Marshall and I escaped. Daddy sent me binoculars for my birthday. Why binoculars? So I might see him? Next year he should send a telescope.

The coffee I brought down to the garage with me is cold, but I like the sharp awakening bite on my tongue. The girl I was at fourteen is a dark figure in the distance I've kept. I cannot claim her without shame. She may be mad at her mother, but she is a girl without a father. Her father is on loan to other families. She cannot garner his attention, let alone win his approval. Her stepmother doesn't like it that he has other children to pay for, and he is a man who avoids conflict at all costs. His daughter is the cost.

October 17

Today we did first-aid training instead of assembly. We thumped on rubber mannequins and lifted each other onto stretchers. Tad chose me to be his partner. "Pay attention, little sis," he said, shaking his finger at me. Is this flirting? His fingers are as long as piano keys.

The senior girls are always talking about how you can tell when a man has a big penis. They say long thumbs. I don't think that's what matters to me, but he does have long thumbs.

When we came to the part where he had to splint my leg, his hands trembled when he wrapped my thigh with gauze, and he kept on trembling after that. I could feel him behind me trembling.

October almost sober

I went up to my brother's room tonight during legitimate visiting hours and Tad was there. Marshall left us alone. He raised and wiggled one eyebrow when he shut the door. Tad said, "Hey little sis," but I said, "You don't think of me that way." And all of a sudden he got real serious. "No, I don't," he said. He sat on the bed and patted the place beside him. I could feel he was trembly again. We lay on Marshall's bed and listened to the whole Blue album. A guy who will listen to Joni! !! ! And he sang falsetto too.

Then he kissed me with his swervy lips, and not like he was in any big hurry either. He never stuffed his tongue into my mouth, not like gross old Ken Wiser, who pinned me down in the ivy in our backyard last year. No, Tad sucked my bottom lip softly and tugged on it just the tiniest bit. He must be way more experienced than me, which makes me feel kind of excited and kind of jealous.

On Sunday morning someone taped a "Lay List" on the kitchen door. I was voted "Most Wanted Virgin." Everyone's teasing me about it, but it is cool to have guys think I am a bitchin' babe!

There's something between the composition books, black, glossy, a magazine folded over. It's the *Life Magazine* issue that published "Faces of the Dead: One Week's Toll." Pictures of 227 soldiers in

1969. I remember that I looked into every face. What could I know of war?

Vietnam was the phantasmagoria of our dreams: children curled up in nests of grass blown back by choppers; women and children crouching in water up to their chests wearing grimaces of fear, except for the baby who looked directly into the camera; women crouching over body bags and conical sedge hats in the sand, the drool of their grief silver and suspended like mercury. Young soldiers, our older brothers or uncles, kneeling over their torn-up, shredded comrades, tipping canteens into each other's mouths. We could see how muddy they were, how weary, how lost.

November 9th

Hey diary, you big dork, I've been ignoring you. I bet you can guess why. Almost every night my roommate Liza goes up to Marshall's dorm and Tad comes to my bed. We call it the Switcheroo! At last bell in the smoking area, Tad asks me, "Are you done with your homework, Missy?" How sweet is that? He has been taking everything so slow with me because he is such a gentleman. Last night he moved down my torso, delivering baby kisses on my tummy, but when he slid my legs apart, I sat bolt upright. Unh-unh. Nobody does that. Shh-shh-shh, he whispered, hushing my protest, stroking my corn-silk hair down there until I settled back into the pillows and gave myself to the tingly, slippery, smooth sensations he created in me. I lay back and imagined strewing rose petals on rippling water.

Liza says we will all live together in a big yellow house and grow our own vegetables and press our own cider and the guys will become carpenters and we will sell pies and jams. What about my songwriting? That too! she says. Every Friday and Saturday night in the local café we'll pass the hat. We sing "Our House" together when we're drunk.

December 22

It's Christmas break. Mom gets mad that I go out so much at night with Marshall. Marshall can drive, and she gave him her old Mercury wagon. Tad called, but I was out at a party. We were hill hopping in a

Volkswagen. Woo-hoo, catching some air! Mom told him she thought I was spending the night at a girlfriend's. Sometimes she can be cool like that.

January 3

Back from Christmas break, Tad came to my room the first night. I was excited because I've been on the pill long enough for us to finally do it. We started out listening to the Allman Brothers, lying on my bed. Everything was getting pretty breathy, and I pulled my underwear off. I think maybe I forced it. I pulled him on top of me. There was this moment where he was looking down, straining like he was in pain. Then I was in pain. Ow. My skin groaned. It's never been stretched like that. I don't care how much he spit on it. Even so, I shoved and pushed with my hips like you're supposed to, but I didn't feel much of anything, more like I'd fallen onto the crossbar of my brother's 10-speed.

I broke down and cried because it never got any good. And Tad kept patting my back and it was annoying, like he was trying to burp a baby doll. And he didn't say anything. I guess I blew it by crying so much. When Tad went to sleep I reached into the place between the bunk bed and the wall. That's where I keep my baby koala, right there stuffed in the crack. I rubbed his soft fur under my chin until I fell asleep.

I have to close the journal for a moment, stare hard at the stuffed animals zipped into plastic cases, the dollhouse on the top shelf. I could unpack these things that belong to my daughter, but I cannot reach my hands through time to be a mother to myself. Above my head is a place where the ceiling has been water damaged and cut out. There's a brown ring the size of a bathtub over my head. In other places the ceiling is covered in black, sooty spots. I don't know whether someone was working on a car in here or trying to kill themselves.

Noelle recently told me she could have gotten in with the

popular kids at school if she'd been willing to party or have sex. We were making a pie together, slicing the cold butter into the flour.

"Who wants to be horny and paranoid?" She shrugged. "Besides, at parties people throw up."

"Tell them you've already done drugs. If intravenous adrenalin isn't an extreme high, I don't know what is."

"Yeah, Mom, and you'd know." We smirk at each other in an exaggerated way, one of our little trademarks. "Guys tell me they want to be my fuck buddy all the time."

She's packing the coarse crumbs into a ball at the center of the bowl.

"That's sexual harassment," I say.

"No, it's just public school. I'd rather be lonely."

I sigh, though I think I have at least done one thing right. I haven't raised a pleaser or placater.

"Do you think it's all the porn the guys are watching?"

"Porn's not even a thing, Mom. Girls watch it too."

I get the wax paper out, and we refrigerate the ball of dough. Maybe her era isn't so far from mine, I think, Lay List and all.

I read on.

Dark daze in January

Tad didn't come to my room last night. Today I couldn't stand it anymore, so I went by his room. He acted like he was happy to see me, but he wouldn't put his guitar down, and what am I supposed to say? He was playing the most depressing song in the world, "Needle and the Damage Done."

"Is something the matter?" I asked him.

"Yeah," he said, "no one heard from my brother over the holidays. My dad filed a missing-persons claim. I think my brother's plane went down in South America." Tad made a sound like a Roman candle, squealing then falling.

"All she wrote, man," he said. I went over to hug him, but he wouldn't put the guitar down, and my rings banged on the wood. "I'm

not feeling so hot," he said. "My dad took me for tests, showed I had mono."

Then the dinner bell rang.

                                                                January rain, mud, rain
Tad didn't come to my room all last week, then last night he was partying up the canyon with the senior girls, swigging Jack and singing drinking songs. He was banging on his guitar, not strumming it at all. Harmony was hanging all over him. He was singing some song all about "lovin' the ladies." Then I stepped up closer, and he said, "Whoa, little sis, I didn't see you there." Heidi the Hassler said, "Sing something G-rated," and they all laughed. I was steamed. I made my way up canyon and drank with every group I came to after that. At the White Log, at Razor Boar Rock, at the Water Tower. Grape juice and gin, Bacardi 151 and Coke, ginger ale and whiskey, tequila sunrises. I got so wasted I fell off a ledge and rolled down into the creek bed. Now my hair feels like a wool blanket that got put in the dryer, dusty, full of stickers and thistle.

Liza is combing my hair out with coconut balsam cream rinse. When the "Lay List" came out this morning, it said, "Tad, on the Uptown Shuttle." That can only mean that he is sleeping with the senior girls. I am crying so much my pen won't work.

"At least you weren't on the list," says Liza. She's only been on it one time because she and Marshall are so steady. It said, "Liza and Marshall, Prom Pussy and Dick King."

"You go ahead and cry," Liza says. "He had no reason to break your heart."

Marshall says Tad still loves me, he is just scared. "Of what?" I shouted.

"I don't know, Maeve," my brother said gently, like he was breaking bad news. "Sometimes you're pretty intense."

The thing is, I don't know how to be less intense.

She doesn't know it yet, but she will need her intensity, once she figures out how to apply it. If I'd become a lawyer instead of a paralegal, I would have had to summon all my intensity to argue in court, sometimes to resist my own emotions as well as the intimidation of opposing counsel. Maybe Noelle will choose something more peaceful, but I doubt it. I stare now at the boxes of Christmas decorations that have made I-don't-know-how-many moves with me, each one marked Fragile. Ghosts of Christmas Past.

We thrived on the stories of the supernatural around us, the little red-haired girl with a tin pail in her hand, seen in the hallways at night, a wisp of a thing who rounded corners, whose crying was heard in the hills. Rumor had it that a plane had gone down in the cove next to ours sometime in the late fifties, and on it a little red-haired girl.

February, endless rain

Last night I woke up, and Leo was sitting by my bed, staring at me. "Shit," I said, "what are you doing here?" "I'm high," he said. "I took some L, and I can't come down." Leo has eyes like a priest's, like he will forgive everything another person does to him and still love them. I told him that, and then we talked for a couple hours. His parents are sailing a sloop in the South Pacific, which I thought was way cool, but he said no it wasn't, because they were only in love with each other and farmed him out on relatives. "Well," I said, "at least they're not divorced."

"Do you think I could get in bed with you?" he asked. I told him I was still hung up on Tad, which he totally understood, and then I let him . . .

Sometimes I see Tad coming out of the girl's bathroom late at night. It's not even funny. In the smoking area he keeps playing "Needle and the Damage Done." I know his brother came back from Vietnam addicted and dealing, but does anybody else know?

I can't take the cold of the garage much longer. I stand and stretch, then take a parka off the coatrack in the corner. It's a huge stadium jacket I wear in the snow—beige and battered. I call it the baked potato. I wonder if Tad ever found his brother. The death toll doesn't end when the war does. We know that now, so many suicides after Iraq and Afghanistan.

Our island was not without reminders of war: batteries and bunkers up on the headlands. On Battery Hill the Army Signal Corps had hunkered down during World War II. There was no radar anymore, only a squat stucco box and the housing for the big transmitter, but some students claimed they could see the concave receiver sweeping the sky on moonlit nights.

March, score some sunshine!
The girls in my dorm decided to be our own cheerleading team. We're
making up our own cheers. Here is what we have so far:

We are the girls from the Salbatora whore core.
We are the ones that the boys pay more for.
Oh listen in them bushes,
to them shoves and pushes,
but you can't call us tramps,
cause we give Blue Chip stamps.

The first spring soccer game, we'd drunk so many rum and Cokes
that we fell down in the grass, in our stupid short skirts, and rolled
around with our pom-poms, laughing, and no one could stop us.

I think of Noelle's slumber parties. Girls screaming, giggling, and dancing until the floorboards buck, episode after episode of hormonal drama, except they are safe, here with me. When I was twelve the babysitter got us stoned. When I was fourteen I stuck out my tongue and someone put a tab of window pane on it, and I smiled as I swallowed. What did I remember of the endless party? I experienced states of the ecstatic. I'll risk saying that. A group of us sat on a ledge above the sea and talked for hours about how we would run the world. I proposed a war theme park where everyone who liked killing could go combat each other, a Disneyland for those who craved murder, mayhem, and war. We were all tripping. I saw droplets of light trickling down a web in the air, and that web was everywhere, and I saw how it connected us. There were those moments, but despite the idealism, mob rule broke out.

A girl named Janie, who wanted to be liked so bad it hurt to look into her face, got raving drunk up canyon, and instead of returning to the girls' dorm, she made her way down the hall of the boy's dorm, proceeding methodically enough, door by door. The next day in the smoking area, a group of guys upended her into a trash can. Janie left the island the next day and never came back. I don't recall hearing a single word about it at our school assembly, though my memory is anything but reliable. It's an archive of decomposing film; the layers of celluloid have separated, resulting in missing patches and white or black blotches. I turn to another page.

March madness

No one knows what happened. Everyone says Tad was doing a lot of sunshine tabs. Marshall says the acid was laced with strychnine. I don't know because I couldn't watch the soccer game. I had a fever, and the nurse only let me out of the infirmary to go to my room. Liza says Tad was playing goalie, which he is usually pretty good at, but he kept missing balls, they were flying right past him. Then he sort of went berserk in the goalie box. He got all twitchy, like hornets had flown up his shirt and were biting him, then he tore off his shirt, and he was stomping on it and yelling, "Die motherfucker!" in the middle of the game, and when the ref came up and got in his face, Tad hauled off and socked him, but then he fell down on his knees crying, his face in his hands. Finally someone got Mr. Campbell, his favorite teacher, who was able to lead him off the field.

I tried to sneak back into the infirmary, but the whole gaggle of senior girls was outside, and they wouldn't let me pass, but they weren't mean to me. Harmony, who has hair down to her butt and these Renaissance Faire eyes, was smoking and shaking her head.

"Bad acid, man," she said, "That's what it will do to you."

"What's going to happen?" I asked.

"Oh, he'll come out of it, but I hear his dad is pissed. I don't think that boy is going to be on the island much longer."

It took me forever to fall asleep, then a loud rain woke me, drumming on the roof. After a while, I realized someone else was breathing with me in the room. Leo was curled up at the foot of the bed under the afghan Grandma crocheted, right there at the foot of the bed like a dog. I pressed my feet against his back and rocked him back and forth. "What are you doing?" I said when he woke up.

"I took a tab of that same acid as Tad," he said. "I don't want to be alone if I go crazy."

"Well, you're not crazy," I said. "You're making my feet go to sleep."

"Can I get in? Please?"

Why can't I say no? What's the matter with me?

He's all about sticking it in, tries to turn me on with his fingers, but he ends up mashing my pee hole, so I pretend I'm really turned on to get it over with. I like the time after the best, when he holds me.

March something

Mom calls on Sundays, sends shoeboxes full of cookies. This week I was glad to hear her voice.

In history class I passed a note to Doug, who sits next to me. "Did Oedipus Rex have casual sex?" In English, we had to write haiku. This time Doug passed me a note.

The sleep from my eye
falls on your pillow.
An ant carries it away.

Leo came to my room again last night. His acne is really bad. It's on his neck. I opened my shoebox of cookies and we pigged out. I don't know how to tell him that I don't want him to come to my room anymore. He's such a sad sack. Why did I sleep with him again?

I stop reading and shut my eyes; before me I see Leo's pitted, loveable face. The island is like an apparition rising in me. I see it as though I were approaching from the water—rock outcroppings, the pebbly beach, a white building with red trim, the boathouse, dories upside down on their racks, hunks of seaweed drying on gray stones. More than memory, the familiar topography of land and heart takes shape inside me.

April No Fool's Day—*Hello Cowgirl in the Sand*
Leo keeps coming into my room at night. I wake up because he is staring at me. I swear his eyes are these swallowing blobs. They're darker than the dark. His face is cratered and zitty, and his nose is shaped like an Evinrude outboard engine, a clunk on his face. The girls don't make fun of him because of his stare, but none of them will sleep with him either.

"Why can't you sleep?" I asked him.

He told me his older brother came back from Vietnam, and last summer he climbed way high up in the mountains, and there was this crag, really steep, and he jumped off it. But the thing is, he didn't die.

"Whoa. He didn't die?"

"No, man," Leo said. "He landed on this ledge below, and he had to jump off again. You could tell because of the bloody handprints."

"Is he dead?"

"Yeah, totally," Leo said.

Then out of nowhere he says, "The people around here do too many drugs," and he starts hitting himself on the head with closed fists. "Come here," I said, but he climbed over me to face the wall. I rubbed his back and hugged onto him until morning, when I guess we must have rolled over because when I woke up I could feel this big boner pressed into my spine. He always wants to and I always let him. Am I a slut?

"Some slut, like you . . ." my daughter said. What was I really, back then? A mental-health professional in the making? A drug-and-alcohol detox bed? A suicide-prevention pussy? I have no words with which to tell my daughter of these exchanges.

Ghosts are trapped on islands; they can't leave. You could hear the feral cats fighting at night, unearthly screams. There were so many island cats that had been abandoned and turned wild, starting with the mousers who rode in on the Spanish ships. There was a ghost story about a rangy, orange tabby that one boy started feeding. Her appetite was prolific despite her scrawniness. The cat took to coming through the open window at night and leaving the remainder of its nocturnal feeding on the desk—voles, rats, baby possums.

The carnage was too much, so the boy put away the cat food and shut the window. But it was Indian summer, October, and he opened the window again. The cat woke the boy by pouncing on his head, strapping her brawny arms around his skull, and sinking her teeth into his scalp before he flung her off.

He enlisted the help of his friend. They bagged the tabby with a pillowcase and took turns swinging the snarling sack in circles as they walked the back road behind the faculty homes and the boathouse, straight out to the end of the pier. The cat emitted a steady, low growl as they tied the brick to the bag, and she shrieked as she felt herself airborne and falling some thirty feet to the water. A trail of bioluminescence marked her descent to the ocean floor.

Perhaps they stayed a little too long, staring with relief at the dark water, and then they saw it, a small cloud of phosphorescence forming, bestirring itself into forward motion, progressing inexorably toward the beach.

"No fucking way, man."

"Creep me the fuck out!"

When at last she reached the shore, they agreed: "We gotta go down there, man." Yet neither of them moved, though the wind gusted stronger in their faces.

"Shit man, I don't want to be part of your bad karma."

Then they went together, hurrying because a high tide was rolling in, and they knelt beside the sodden sack, working a Swiss Army knife through the wet knots while the cat mewled. Once the sack was open, they scrambled back to the road and watched her emerge, looking much like the carcasses she'd left. Later they swore she still came at night to sit on the window ledges and glare. You can't escape memory; it drags the brick in the deep.

April is the cruelest month

Tad doesn't answer my letters. He is shining me on. He's in a new school on the mainland. I won't let myself cry anymore.

Later

There was a huge school party with half a pound of weed and 21 cases of beer. Radical Richard (a senior!) took me to this place up the canyon. There are these cargo nets tied way up in the eucalyptus trees. I was scared to climb wearing zories on that slat ladder. Some of the rungs only have one nail stuck into the tree. But we made it all right, even though he got bong water down his pants. "Serves you right," I said, and next thing I know we are tumbling to the center of the net, and he tells me I am a prick tease. Is that true? I gave him head so he would stop groping me. I still don't know what to do about Leo. He woke me up again this morning with his staring. It's starting to freak me out.

Spring break where are you?

I told Leo he can't come to my room anymore because I'm Richard's woman now. He cried. Sometimes I wonder if the only reason I loved my mom's boyfriends was for her. When she said it was time to go, it was time to go. I felt sadder about leaving my cat than leaving her last boyfriend. Telling Leo he had to go made me feel like a cold person.

If I shut my eyes I feel my feet once more in the silt of the canyon trail. Did I see fox eyes shimmer green in the brush, or was I just imagining it? Salbatora Island had its own species. In the warm rain we wended our way toward the logs and eucalyptus groves that served as our gathering places. I smelled sage, mustard, and fennel in the wet heat. Chicory, goldenrod, coyote brush—we dissolved into the smell of night. High up the canyon, boys rolled boulders, levered them up and sent them crashing and thumping their way down the canyon walls. Except one night a boy named Stuart wanted to join their gang, and he headed up after. Who knew he was coming? A rolling boulder cracked his skull, and he was flown off island to get a plate put in his head. Like the others who disembarked, we heard no more of him. Is it any wonder I don't attend reunions, don't chummy up on Facebook to partake of nostalgia?

When my mother moved on I learned to let people fall through trapdoors. Perhaps I am a cold person. According to Noelle right now, I'm merciless. The garage smells slightly of methane and fiberglass insulation. I stayed married for fifteen years to a man whose parents saw their fiftieth wedding anniversary. At some point for me habit replaced love, though I can't pinpoint where this happened on the timeline, and habit wasn't enough. But I am a loyal and generous parent, sister, daughter, friend, lover—and I think I make the Best Ex-Wife in the World, if there is a title for that. My ex and I exchange Christmas gifts, attend recitals together, and when his mother died I cooked a roast. Does this make me a good model to my daughter? Better than a long-suffering wife? I read on, suffering the same dread with which one reads a last bequest, to find out if it will reward or punish. Or both. Both is the more realistic possibility.

May up and away
I've never hung out with Henry, but he wanted to hike up the canyon
after English class. He was all excited about Aldous Huxley because
the guy wrote a book about an island. So I wrote the quote down, and
we finished a doobie.

It's like an electric current. . . . But luckily, the wire carries no messages. One touches and, in the act of touching, one is touched. Complete communication but nothing communicated. Just an exchange of life, that's all.

Henry said he was going to be a famous musician, and I told him I would write all the lyrics. "You're so beautiful," he said. "You're like Sylvia Plath." Then we got stoned, and I walked into the creek wearing my shoes. I am so sad to be leaving all my friends. Then Henry wanted to do it in the back of the maintenance truck, but the metal was too hot and we didn't have a blanket.

June 1st and last on this island
I woke up because of Leo again. He said ghosts were after him.

He was really tripping. He told me he was afraid, that his doppelgänger was going to push him off the cliff. I told him it was just because we finished reading *The Secret Sharer* last week. We didn't even know what a doppelgänger was before that. He seemed to calm down after that. But I let him get in bed with me again. Then later a bunch of guys went down the hallway yelling, "Let's get rowdy!" and banging on every door. Mine popped open, and Leo jumped up naked to close it. "Whoa," someone yelled. "Leo's getting it on with Maeve." Then Heidi the Hassler screamed at them to get the fuck out.

This morning, Hang Dog Harmony leaned on my doorframe. She told me I better go look at the "Lay List." I put my cowboy boots on right in front of her and stomped out wearing my flannel Tyrolean nightgown. I found my name in the middle of the list. It said, "Maeve, the Whore of Healing." At least I wasn't first; that was "Sue, Most Saddlesore." I was blubbering in front of the kitchen door when Mr. Campbell came up to tear it down. "You shouldn't pay any attention to that," he said, and he hugged me in a just nice way.

I close the journal on my thumb. The memory of myself at fourteen is enough to shake the day off its foundation. It's noon already, and I haven't made it from the garage to the office I keep in the house. I shove the box of journals back behind the propane camp stove and make my way back upstairs. On the landing I am overtaken by an image of myself as a girl. I don't know if I am remembering this or making it up. That night I didn't go to the canyon or the boys' dorm, and I left my own room empty. I climbed the hill to the battery, the tang of tansy and yarrow full in my nostrils, animals moving in the brush, thistles catching on the hem of my nightgown. I heard the far-off sound of the sea, rushing forward and rearing back. I walked the battery in my long nightgown with the periwinkle flowers on it, not knowing if I wanted to be seen as a ghost or if I had already become one.

At four o'clock my daughter announces her arrival by dropping her backpack on the landing. She calls out for me, seeking my whereabouts in the house. "Mom? Mahmmmm?" I let the sound of her voice find me, not because I am feeling contrary but because that note of need is so seldom struck these days. "There you are," she says, stopping at the doorframe, a gloriously leggy creature with hair falling across her shoulders.

"I'm sorry about this morning. I didn't mean for it to come out that way."

"It really did hurt my feelings."

"I didn't actually call you a slut, Mom. I said, 'At least I don't behave like a slut.'"

She is reiterating the distinction of twenty parenting books: Address your child's behavior. Don't call names or label.

"Let's leave it at that," I say. "I accept your apology."

She pops her heels out of her shoes and kicks them expertly into the corner behind my door. "I get it, Mom. More than you think. Some of the popular girls text pictures of themselves in their underwear to their boyfriends."

"Are they wearing bras?"

"No, Mom, that's the whole point of sexting. But they don't get it that the guys are sharing the pictures and getting off on it."

"I'm glad you have a good head on your shoulders," I say. "You don't have to please them."

"No shit, Sherlock. You raised me to be feisty."

"Yes," I say, "we practice a lot."

"Oh yeah," she says, sailing out of my office to get a snack. "We practice a lot."

ANYTHING BUT THAT

| | | | | | | | | | | | | | | | | | | | | | | | | | | |

U p to now we've had a marriage made in Costco. That was our joke about the day Walter put me on his Costco membership, and I had my picture taken for the ID card. What followed was a mature discussion of marriage.

"It's the concept that bothers me," Walter said. "You start out as a half looking to become a whole." His hand rested warmly on my thigh while we drank our cheap berry smoothies in the car.

"Yes," I said with a little gasp because I'd sucked in too much liquid and given myself a brain freeze. "The lack. It's kind of like original sin."

"And then the concept of marriage becomes the third entity."

"I know. You don't want to rock the boat, so you stop telling the truth."

Right there in the Costco parking lot, amid sweet-faced, big-assed Americans lying in stores for the zombie apocalypse, we decided that if we ever got married, we would remain truth tellers. We loved each other constantly and infinitely if not unconditionally.

It was all well and good until I had a couple of intermediate cancers carved out of my back, and Walter developed high blood pressure, and my own father's sudden death had left its mark. My dad, who walked four miles the day before he died, suddenly dropped dead from a massive heart attack.

"I guess that was the number of breaths he had in him," my yoga teacher said.

It seems every six months or so Walter and I hear about an acquaintance who goes to the doctor with some mild complaint and comes home with a death sentence. I'm beginning to feel lucky. I may have Crohn's disease, but if I spend my weekends quietly, I can usually get back in remission in time for Monday morning.

I know I am trying to spur Walter toward marriage as a way of inoculating myself against further illness, but I can't seem to stop myself. Even though he is the sweetest, funniest man I know. Last year's cancer surgery left me white-coat phobic. Now I can't put on any gown that opens in the back, not even at Macy's, and especially not the paper kind you wear for a pap smear.

Walter suggested I keep my dress on and tell the doctor, "You can pull my panties aside, but that's it."

After that I told my daughter, "Find a man who is amused by you." Better to laugh away the years than gripe and swipe your way through them.

Who is griping now? Up until last night Walter and I were having a perfectly fine weekend. Now it's Monday, and I'm looking beyond the crumbling windowsill at his fruit-laden plum tree, opulent and pendulous, and his flame roses, fiery and creamy at the same time. After we've had a fight I like to run it back through my mind like a film spool, but with the volume off, so that it looks vaudeville funny: me, the belligerent one stomping backward out of the room while Walter flails his arms in reverse. I'm sure this is not constructive behavior by the standards of any advice on how to stay married, and we're not even married yet.

"Please don't wreck our happiness by focusing on the one thing you think is wrong," Walter said, "when so much is right." I think of my friends who remain single despite professing to want a mate. Is their singlehood the result of men trading in for younger models, or is that a myth? Are women my age too critical of men? Less tolerant about the cowboy boots on the coffee table or whatever the proverbial equivalent is?

I look at the kitchen counter where his empty wine glass stands, residual maroon rings at its center, blooming like a peony. He likes to swirl his wine, *volatizing* is the word he taught me. On Sunday I heard the roar of the football game in the other room, the little gasp of the cork in spite of the sports announcers' exhortations to the winning team on the TV. It started out as nothing.

"Are you drinking in the afternoon?" I shouted from the bedroom, even though I know everybody drinks on game day.

"No, I'm practicing my Russian."

I heard the squeegee of the cork going back in. "There, I put it away. You happy?"

"This time, maybe."

"Oh, go take one of your pills."

"Which prescription?" I hummed a few bars from "The Battle Hymn of the Republic." "The one that knocks me out?"

"*Some* women would be glad their man was out of their hair for a few hours." His tone was mock hurt, and he drew out the vowels.

"Some women," I said. "But I'm not one of them."

"You're in a class by yourself, baby. Come here."

"No, I'm working."

"You expect *me* to get up?"

This is what we sound like most of the time—two kids poking each other in the stomach. Although I divorced in my early forties—and according to all the polls that put fear in your future, I had a bullfrog's chance in a well of finding a prince—I had found a sweetheart. Well, not found him exactly, because he'd been there all along, but I'd been too stupid to notice. I'd ruled Walter out, originally because he belonged to someone else, and later I forgot to notice him again. This was before I realized I wanted a man who could be a boon companion, not some smoldering hulk who needed his emotions translated. I wanted someone who already spoke the language, who could talk with me about all the characters in a movie and what each one's motive was. Walter was like that. He talked as much as my girlfriends did. And when I told him I was taking a mood stabilizer, he said, "So? The world is wobbling a little more on its axis, too." My generation "tried to have it all" without the support envisioned by seventies feminism. Now when people ask, "How did you manage?" I want to answer, "It helps to be a little manic."

This love affair with Walter is relatively recent: four years, but the taproot goes deep—he was married to my college friend Maureen. The couple ran a catering business right after graduation. They even catered my wedding to Guy. I remember leaning against the kitchen counter and watching how fast he chopped in the direction of his own fingers. He shooed me away. "If I cut off my finger, it will ruin your dress." I always found Walter to be a merrymaker, a raconteur, a man who liked feast and fest. At parties I cozied up to him in the kitchen. One child and ten years later, his wife Maureen tore her scapula chopping vegetables and went to Maui to convalesce, where she met somebody. Then she left Walter to become a trophy wife. Last time I saw Maureen she was on the sidelines at a basketball game wearing a tennis visor and black capris, surrounded by other women wearing tennis visors and white capris. Her toenails were wine red, and she wore gold toe rings, and she made a parade wave at me but never came over to talk. Neither did I. Walter, for his part, raised their son faithfully, occasionally dating younger women who punished him roundly with their little tantrums by leaving the party or leaving the country. I, on the other hand, only leave the room. My kids like me better when I'm with him; they know I have backup now. What's really best for their young lives is not to have to think about me at all.

This afternoon I am alone in his cluttered little house where piles of books and magazines rise up from the living-room floor like miniature high-rise buildings. When Walter left to meet with clients, he did not give me his customary kiss. What was he supposed to do? I slept on the couch last night. The olive-green blankets are lumped up on the armrest and vaguely suggest the shape of Babar the Elephant. I am supposed to be finishing a legal brief and packing, not sulking and skulking about.

I called him a barnacle last night. I meant to sound like I was teasing, but the words were scorched when they came out, charry around the edges. I guess I am trying to goad him into moving up north. "You're a goddamn barnacle," I said. Very mature lead-in. That started the fight about getting married. I want him to pack up his house and move into mine, which happens to be six hundred miles north of Oakland in a suburb of Seattle. I finished the paralegal program at Edmonds Community College, then I secured a good job with benefits for a domestic law firm, and I typed up my own divorce from Guy and his papers, too. I'm ready. I want to be with Walter, but I sense something lugubrious in him, sludgy. Could it be the sheer stuffage in his garage? He comes from a family of immigrants who lived in a displaced persons camp after World War II. When your family has lost everything, you throw away nothing. Perhaps it is only his careful, protective nature, the very same that makes me feel so loved. In any case he responded to the barnacle comparison in a formal, meted-out fashion that meant I had hurt his feelings.

"You're right," he said. "Love between barnacles is difficult. The organisms cannot leave their shells to mate."

"Don't talk to me in metaphors."

"I'm not. This is why I keep all those *National Geographics* that you want to throw away. Barnacles have extraordinarily long penises. I bet you didn't know that. In fact, barnacles probably have the largest penis to body size ratio in the animal kingdom."

"Well, your penis cannot get to me if we live six hundred miles apart. It's not that long. I want us to live together." This from the woman who told him she would make an art out of missing him until he could retire.

"I thought we were talking about getting married."

"Same deal."

"Not true. Some people have commuter marriages and live together part-time."

I felt the subject getting away from me. I had the sensation that I was trying to cram a large wad of paper into a tiny envelope.

"Is that what you're proposing?"

"No," he said. "I'm not proposing anything."

"Precisely." I felt my unreasonableness reaching its poetic pitch. I was the winter witch sweeping in on a frosty breath. It felt marvelous.

"Why now?" he asked.

"Why not?" I countered.

He sighed audibly. "I know I want to spend the rest of my life with you," he said. "Isn't that enough?"

"Not after four years." There, I'd toted up the years, and doing so made me feel righteously right.

"You said you wanted to wait until Noelle moved out."

"Well, she's finishing her AA degree now, and she's going to UW in the fall. So don't let her keep you."

"Maeve," he said with forbearance, "we've been planning our future together. When I retire, I can move to Seattle full-time."

He did not sound like he was cajoling or bargaining. Infuriating. "Why should I have to convince you to marry me?" I screeched. Dreadful noise. "You're commitment phobic!" The phrase sounded like some bullet point in one of the women's glossies under the heading, "Will He or Won't He?"

"Is this a deal breaker?" he asked.

"I don't know," I said. "It could be."

Today I can't tell if I am reacting to things Walter said because of things my ex-husband said, and if I reacted to those things because of things my father once said. Shit. It's a tough go, being ding-and-dent models. Walter and I come "as is" after previous lives. What I love about Walter, besides his perfectly punctuated emails, is his flair for improvisation, his abundant silliness. If we hadn't fought last night, his return from the university office of event planning would have been the perfect occasion for us to pretend we were in a telenovela. "El Señor es en la casa!" he would announce with mock severity, slamming the door slightly. "El hermano de ley está en el armario." The brother-in-law is in the closet, I would say in a high, breathy voice. Then he would stomp loudly across the living room, and I would screech when he found me, and we would carry on together.

Now what? Do I have to break up with him because he won't marry me? Or did he even say that? Did he say he wouldn't marry me? Maybe he will marry me after he moves up north; maybe we will marry each other if I put down the gun I'm holding to his head. I pace the house. In a few hours he will come home from work to give me a ride to the airport, and I don't know how to fix it between us. On my second swing through the kitchen, I slap the cupboard doors shut (he told me once I was like living with a poltergeist because I fling the cupboards open and leave them that way). My teabag wrappers flutter to the floor.

I skinny into the small space between my side of the bed and the wall, grabbing my books from the bed stand. When he comes to my house, he leaves a pair of glasses on the nightstand, as though he were coming to bed presently. I usually leave a book, but now I gather all of them. One of the books in my hands is a compendium of marriage vows. I thought we would read through it together, but no, that isn't going to happen.

I thumb through it now in a masochistic fury. Protestants first. *The bond and covenant of marriage was established by God in creation, and our Lord Jesus Christ adorned this manner of life by his presence and first miracle at a wedding in Cana of Galilee.* Right . . . the wedding in Cana. Christ changed the water into wine, thereby resolving the first catering crisis. I'd seen the Renaissance painting in the Louvre, *The Wedding Feast at Cana.* Napoleon had ordered it brought to Paris from a Benedictine monastery, which involved cutting the painting in half and stitching it back together. There it was again, those two halves. The wedding in the painting is extravagant, crowded with over a hundred guests, but not one is featured speaking. The Benedictines liked their vow of silence. Good for the in-laws.

The actual vows seem to set off in the same fashion, with God as the first wedding guest—*we have come together in the presence of God.* I don't mind that. The presence of God can be a meteor shower, or the incandescent blue of a glacial crevasse, or the indwelling God that tells you you've been a nasty bitch to your perfectly loving partner. There, I used the word *partner* again. People assume we are a lesbian couple when I put it on paper, "Maeve Beaufort and partner." They assume two women are showing up. Good-bye Walter Tabakov. How ironic: heterosexual couples are adopting a lesbian vocabulary and fleeing the institution of marriage at the historic moment that gay couples feel it is a victory to be allowed marriage.

I have reached the Catholic vows, which don't really seem to require the presence of women. *What God has joined, men must not divide.* I picture women on burros or camels, the animals' halter ropes pulled upon by men, fathers, or husbands, it doesn't matter. For thousands of years women came to marriage as chattel. Even now the guest list is stacked with men: *in the name of the father, and of the son, and of the Holy Spirit.* Still, the language is elegantly wrought and rings with solemnity of purpose. *Eternal God look with favor upon the world you have made, and especially this man and this woman.* This is a blessing I long for. I suffer from this terrible fear that now that Walter and I are free at last to love each other, one of us will be struck down before we can ever actually live together.

It's a thorny thicket, wanting to be married but not liking the vows. I believe in loyalty and devotion; you can agree to see each other to the heavenly door without giving up selfhood entirely. Yet I cannot answer the question in the affirmative: *Have you come freely and without reservation to give yourselves to each other in marriage?* The trouble is I believe in keeping my reservations, as a healthy tension on the line. And he can keep his, too, for that matter. For so many, marriage seems to be the grand gesture that absolves one of further effort. Is it fine to ignore the temple God gave you, your body? To sink into the La-Z-Boy, to refuse the physical therapist's exercises and make everyone else cut your toenails? Is a little bit of worry about staying healthy and attractive to your mate such a bad thing if it keeps a thousand and one bad behaviors in check? I thought "unconditionally" was supposed to refer to anything you couldn't prevent. It doesn't give you a free pass to become a slob.

My grandmother once said to me, "I never imagined I'd become a nurse with a purse," though she stayed with her second husband, who was a testy, short-tempered man. I did notice that if he went too far, my grandmother would hold up one finger like an elementary school teacher and fix it in front of his face, and he would back down. I wish I knew what that one finger meant.

Maybe it isn't too late to convert to Judaism. Those vows are better. *Blessed are you unnamable God, source of the universe who created woman and man in your image and placed eternity in their hearts.* This speaks to me; eternity has already been placed in our hearts, and our vows will be a recognition that this sublime thing has already taken place.

Last night was anything but sublime. "I'm not creating a conflict when there isn't one," I said. "You're avoiding the subject."

"I'm not avoiding the subject. There are practical matters to consider. If I leave now, my retirement will take a hit, whereas two years from now—"

"Don't even say that. Don't say two years from now." And so on and so forth it went.

I notice that the Buddhist vows mention anger. *Courtesy and consideration even in anger and adversity are the seeds of compassion. Love is the fruit of compassion.* Oh no . . . this is the big one: *We take full responsibility for our own life in all its infinite dimensions . . . We are committed to embrace all parts of ourselves, including our deepest fears and shadows, so we can be transformed into light.* It's a call to a high order of love all right. I cast a glance toward the phone, but I'm too mad to dial his number, and it isn't going to ring just because I look at it, so I place the book of vows with the others in my suitcase, underneath my shoes. Vow or no vow, today Walter is the better woman.

I look about the house for some penance I can perform. Organize his books? No, I'll start reading them as I sort them. Clean the bathroom? I definitely feel my greatest resistance there. I arm myself with gloves, brush, and Bab-O.

It is a threshold to consider . . . the first time you clean a man's toilet. Must it signify submission? I wonder, since chances are he'll never notice it, though the smell up close is as pungent as a pissoir in Paris. It's my deal, I rationalize. *Don't expect applause.* Isn't that a Buddhist expression? I'll do it for myself. The choice of where and how I plant my ass is my dominion, after all, and therefore not degrading. Because I am not his *wife*, this is not a permanent designation or duty. I am here on holiday, for a long weekend.

Like yolk slopped over the edge of an egg, urine trails runnel down the outside of the toilet's basin. I must face myself here, at the underside of the bowl, where the S-shaped porcelain finds egress, goes underground. Not a pretty place for reflection, the underside of the bowl, not one where memories of Alexander torte and champagne hold up for long. Oh no, not down here in the dribble and dirt, the dead moth wings.

I am not prepared to see my mouth stretch open in the chrome bolt covers as I wipe up hair stuck in urine. Is this the meaning of the Buddhist wedding vow, *I take you to be my equal in love, as a mirror for my true self.* My true self is butt-ugly from down here. The cleaning supplies are raising a ring of welts around my mouth.

But I commit myself to this act of humility, of lowering myself, and I spray and erase the besplatterment around the rim, chastising myself for being bourgeoisie. If I were a true beatnik, I'd spit in the bowl, throw cigarette butts at it.

The *wife* kills the adventurer every time. Haven't I learned that? Escaped domestication in favor of the feral? Gloria Steinem said, "I don't mate in captivity." Do I really want Walter calling me "his wife?" Or worse yet, "the wife?" "The wife this and the wife that." Yada yada. The men guffaw. "You know how the wife feels about that." Hardy har har. Maybe they have those little plaques with witticisms above the kitchen sink: "I'm the boss around here, and if you don't believe me, just ask my wife." Or I can join the lawyers' wives eating and complaining at cocktail parties, "My husband thinks he knows how to fix the plumbing . . . Well, my husband . . ." It's a dumb and dumber contest. Do Walter and I want to be claimed by all these clichés?

The sewer treatment plant claims that it discharges *effluent* into the bay; you have to marvel at how the word *shit* can be transformed into something as poetic as *effluent*. Better to stick with the word *shit*, close to the source, and *fuck* for the same reason. It isn't that I don't love Walter; I love him most of all. And often we do *make love*, but sometimes I want to say what I mean, I want to say what I need. Then we fuck each other silly, laughing afterward at our mad middle-aged exertions.

Ye gods, the bowl is mildewed on the back side between the pipe and the wall. I spray bleach solution copiously and swab with paper towels. I keep myself amused by thinking of Seattle's founding fathers, who built the town so close to the Puget Sound that high tide blasted those tycoons right off their thrones. Enough already. The bleach solution is dripping down my wrists and back inside the gloves. Abruptly I stand, banging the crown of my head against his shaving mirror, which extends from the wall on an expando arm. As I shove it away, the mirror falls out and shatters into the toilet. I kneel to pick out the magnified pieces of my face.

Scrubbing his toilet has altered our relationship, I am sure of it, though I wouldn't venture to say *how*. But at least when he comes home I will have the wit not to ask him to notice his nice clean toilet and thank me for it. I hear the creak of the front door and stare down at the last of the mirror shards.

"Honey, I'm home," Walter shouts in an exaggerated tone.

"I cleaned the bathroom," I shout back, "as a way of doing penance."

"Good. Then you've only got a few Hail Marys to go."

"I'm sorry," I say. "I broke your mirror, and I'm fishing my face out of the toilet."

"Not that," Walter says. "I can handle anything but that."

WHO WILL LOVE ME NOW?

| | | | | | | | | | | | | | | | | | | | | | | | | | | | | | | | | |

I am on Walter's ancient couch that bears his permanent butt marks and always makes me wonder who all he might have fucked on these very cushions. It will be the first thing to go when we move in together. It's 2:00 a.m., and I am stationed here because it is close to the bathroom, and I don't want to wake Walter. I wonder if Crohn's disease is like having trichinosis from eating undercooked polar bear meat, which happened to those polar explorers whose balloon went down over the Arctic Sea. In my case, it's revenge of the guacamole from last night. The lime juice and cayenne pepper. "It's mild," Walter said. "At least try it." I should have known better. I can't eat to please anyone. So now I am up late considering the fate of nineteenth-century polar explorers who didn't have gastroenterologists.

Another trip to the loo. After being eaten, the trichinosis larvae release from their cysts and invade the wall of the small intestine. Not many would consider it a privilege to know the shape of the bowel. The term "loo" may come from the French, *lieux d'aisances*, places of ease. Not for me, not today . . . I swear I can feel the larvae developing into adult worms, the vague burning sensation of something burrowing into my flesh.

Evidently, I have left my "distress tolerance skills" at home along with my emergency pack of prednisone, Canasa suppositories, cortisteroidal suppositories, and extra Pentasa. My mindful acceptance of primary suffering (the flare-up) that allows me to avoid secondary suffering (aversion, resistance, and resentment) can go fuck itself. The worms are growing longer. Tummy rumble. Another trip. Fecal violence.

I have noticed myself thinner these last few months, probably malabsorption of the nutrients in food. Women ask me what diet I am on, and some of them would run across the room to catch this disease if it were contagious. I apologized to Walter last night for taking so long to have an orgasm.

He said, "Do you think I want to spend any less time loving you?"

Dear God, I don't want to wake him for *this* process of the body. I am freezing. I rummage in his linen closet and wrap myself in an afghan of many greens. Maybe his mother made it. I turn up the heat. Still, I shake. The couch is my island in a sea of floating icebergs. I hold my hands out in front of me and watch them tremor. Trich from uncooked polar bear meat can cause serious neurological damage when the worms enter the central nervous system. How will Walter know what has happened when he finds me? I've told him about my affliction, but he's never actually seen me sick. Will he still love me when I am so weakened by it I can barely crawl across icy Pitcairn Island to light my lantern? There's a progression to a disease—this one is incurable.

He will have to call the kids, who are finally beginning to accept him.

On New Year's Norman was dropped off by the police, staggering drunk at my front door.

"I *snow* how to talk to cops, Mom." He says cops like a copse of trees, his *s* hanging like slobber from his tongue. "I *toll* the cops about my summer painting graffiti."

I'd gotten Norm into a summer ride-and-work program with the police when he was fourteen, but now hardly seemed the moment to be self-congratulatory.

"Where were you, Norman?" I ask.

"Iz cool, Mmm."

"Goddammit, Norman, who were you with?"

I felt Walter behind me, watchful but not intrusive. Norman

was leaning against the front door, and now he slid across it. When his shoulder hit the wall, he tipped forward like the Tin Man, and Walter stepped up in time to catch him up by his armpits.

"Here, sling an arm over my shoulder."

"Ank you, man." Norm cranked his head to call to me over his shoulder, "Sid got taken away, Mom, cuz he told the cops to fuug off. I din do that . . ."

Through the door I heard bedsprings and hollering and the toilet flushing. Then Noelle was hanging about the front door in her koala bear nightshirt, prurient with pubescent curiosity. "What happened? What happened?"

"Your brother had too much to drink, Ellie, but he'll be fine in the morning."

"I saw the police lights. Are they gonna arrest him?"

She sounded hopeful for a full-on drama in the house. "No, they just brought him home. Now go on back to bed."

"Good thing he won't be eighteen for another month," she called over her shoulder, sashaying down the hall.

I stood by Norman's door and heard more toilet flushing, then Walter's voice. "Everyone gets to visit the porcelain throne sometime . . ."

"Uhh, uhh," followed by grunting and retching noises.

"Take a towel."

I opened the door and saw Walter easing Norman back into bed, but Norm flopped the last few inches, his feet splayed. Norman's voice was slow with emotion, the words heavy. "Ank you, man. I know I act like an asshole. But I luuuve you, man."

Walter looked toward me quickly.

"Don't worry about it," Walter said. "I love you, too, man."

At Walter's house I am self-conscious about flushing the toilet so much, opening and closing the bathroom door. When I come out again I hear a catch in Walter's rumble—I wouldn't call it snoring; more like a steady drone. The earth emits a dronelike sound, and scientists are studying it to find out why. I could spare them the expense. *Because* is what we tell our children when we've run out of explanation, the irrefutable *Because*. On the way back from the water closet, I stop before a hand-painted blanket chest in the hall, a faded urn and garlands scrolling across it. On top sits a jewelry armoire, and the hooks inside the door hold strings of amber, garnets, and rose quartz. I finger the necklaces, wondering if they are his mother's or his grandmother's. There's a row of tiny drawers that Noelle likes to open and shut when she is here.

Noelle, too, came slowly toward Walter, though she bore her father's cudgel. When she was nine and ten, she liked roughhousing with an aggressive edge. At the park she would jump Walter from the back, cut him off at the larynx, lunge at his knees. He shook her off like a bear or spun her till she shrieked and let go. In a diner booth she would punch him in the arm or try to push him out of the booth until I shut her down.

He gave her ways to express her aggression that became inside jokes between them—he showed her how gymnasts in competition give each other insincere air kisses and back pats. This became their standard greeting as they said things like, "Hope you fall off and break your leg." He also taught her the comedy gesture from *The Kids in the Hall* using his thumb and forefinger to sight on people's heads. "I crush your tiny head," she would say from across the room, and he would crush hers too, as if to say, "Annoyance doesn't only run one way, baby." Walter made Noelle's animosity safe. "I can't help but like him," she told me once, looking consternated. But she did not touch him with affection, not for three years, until one day he said something so funny, she walked toward him laughing and he simply opened his arms.

Will my illness now undo all this? If I go to the hospital, Walter will hear every gruesome detail of my bowels. And we have traversed each other's lives so well up to now, the steep of whole histories. When we are apart I buy myself his favorite foods: white nectarines, purple potatoes, gorgonzola. I find a taste for everything he loves. Wait until Walter finds out how boring chronic illness is, like a Monopoly game on a relentless rainy vacation you don't get to go home from. How could I blame him for cutting out now? How could I not blame him? I don't wake him. I forestall the moment. I shudder on this couch like a generator with the choke full open. Who will love me now?

The last time I had a flare-up was after the divorce. At this point I guess I thought happiness had made my illness go away. I remember the nurses placing a sash of yellow tape across my hospital door with the word "Enteric" printed on it over and over, as though I were a crime scene. The doctors kept asking, "Have you been overly stressed?" They invited me to pathologize my life instead of seeing the social problems that have affected it. Like college debt. Like the lack of paid family leave, state-supported child care, or equal pay— the agenda my women's studies class made sound like an inevitability. Back when. Where was rest to be found? The double whammy was our husbands. What did they know but stay-at-home moms?

I remember Noelle at seven, staring at the table mat of vines and berries, saying quietly, "We are never going to be the family in *Little House on the Prairie* again."

That night on the phone, Regina's sarcasm saved me, "Did you tell her, 'You're right. We have indoor plumbing.'"

"Regina!" I squawked, though I was not outraged.

"Sorry, I know, divorce is a stab to the heart. For everybody."

Regina likes to point out that modern American parenting is based on protection, while age-old Jewish parenting is based on survival. "Troubles are to man what rust is to iron," she says and shrugs. "No one gets a perfect life."

After Guy moved out, eleven-year-old Norman stood over my bed, pumping up his scrawny chest in imitation of the Hulk and ripping his pajama top open, the buttons pinging on the hardwood floor. "You're making me pee!" Noelle screamed, running for the bathroom in laughter. There was no one to get mad at us.

"Maeve," I hear Walter call from the bedroom. "Are you all right? You've been up all night."

I focus my surprise on a velveteen dog on the side table whose head waggles. Walter's daughter gave it to him. I smack the dog on the nose just because I can.

"Revenge of the guacamole," I say.

"Can I do something for you?"

"You can take me to the hospital, Walter. I'm not well."

"I'm coming," says Walter. "Let me find my trousers."

In the emergency room two strings of origami cranes hang on either side of the intake desk. Pictures of lighthouses and sea stacks hang above the orange couches. Affixed to the wall is an electronic thermometer holder and a hook from which dangle blood-pressure cuffs.

Ahead of me at the intake desk, a substantial man in black flannel pajamas dotted with pineapples leans against his wife. She is wearing a full-length maroon parka and flannel pajamas too, light blue with teddy bears. Her hair is so long it swings behind her like a shawl. From the back, the man's frizzy gray hair stands out from his pate, David Crosby style. I actually scoffed in the parking lot when I saw the pair ahead of us, knowing Walter and I would be delayed by the slowness of their shuffle, these people who couldn't even get dressed. At the glass window I hear them check in.

She says, "He had surgery on Monday."

He says, "I didn't know where else to go."

The staff got him an exam room—triaged to the top of the list. Over dispatch I hear that they are bringing in a guy who has been hit in the face with a nail gun. I don't know whether that means he has nails in his face or he has been coldcocked. No one clarifies. When the man in the pajamas walks toward the swinging doors, he lifts his whole left side starting with his shoulder in order to gain enough altitude with his leg to lift it from the floor before he pounds his cane in front of him and then crashes down upon the leg with all his weight. Meantime, a ponytailed nurse's assistant has planted a thermometer in my mouth. 103.2. Every joint in my body begs to be uncoupled. The man makes it halfway across the waiting room before he stops. His cane in front of him, Moses-like, he pronounces, "That's it. I can't go no further."

His wife leans in and says something I can't hear, then they take two small sideways steps together and he lowers himself into an outside aisle chair. When the wheelchair comes, its bearer is a young Latina woman with blonde hair in pink clips who stares at the girth of the man in front of her. There is a noticeable moment of hesitation, a downbeat. The man's wife steps into the breach, long hair swinging at his side, their movements practiced—he places the cane in front again, and *heave ho*, on some internal count, she lifts him on the bad-leg side as he lifts the good-leg side, and they arrive at standing, together, looking into each other's faces, flushed as though they had finished a polka, her broad Slavic face beaming with the triumph of lifting him again. I chew on my lips, the lips that a half hour ago were so easy with cursing.

Walter holds my hand; his warmth flows into me. He wraps his coat around my shoulders. I shall miss his consideration, his good manners. I could cry for myself, but I won't. I am practicing forgiveness. Someone is moaning. A teenaged boy holds a bloody hand wrapped in a diaper. Where is his mother? A middle-aged woman in a white uniform leans over her knees, rocking. A man whose back is a question mark lifts his head like a turtle; he holds onto a green oxygen tank as though someone might steal it from him, and the line that snakes up to his nose gleams in the severe light of fluorescent tubes. I shut my eyes. I brought water and Tylenol. After some hours I follow Walter's shoes through the swinging doors. Large, square blocks of sky-blue linoleum alternate with white tile. I have the sensation that the blue blocks are floating, that if I step on a blue tile, it will skid out from underneath me like ice on water. We come to my gurney in the curtained-off room.

A young attending asks me the same questions another attending did a half hour ago. This is a teaching hospital. Her name tag says Maggie and her hair is auburn. I study her eyes. You could not call them brown, though they are loamy soft; there's too much iron oxide in them. They are the color of rust.

"Please list surgeries and/or hospitalization dates." She looks apologetic. Fortunately, I've answered these before, so I am prepared. "C-section, 2000."

"I see you've had two children, but only one C-section."

"Yes, only one C-section."

"The other birth was vaginal."

"Yes, vaginal birth."

Walter looks at me over the top of his magazine. I flare my nostrils at him like Ferdinand the Bull.

"Okay. Other surgeries or hospitalizations . . ."

"Uhh, five years ago, hospitalization for Crohn's."

"How many days?"

"A week."

"Any blockages, abscesses, or fistulas?"

Walter looks at me again. I've always talked about this hospitalization with great finality, in the past, something over and done with.

"None."

"What is your pain level, on a scale of one to ten, with one being little or no pain—"

"And ten being death?" I interject. She looks up at me solemnly from her clipboard.

"No," Walter says. "Ten is wishing you were dead."

Another attending comes in, a different one, with a military-style haircut, high and tight, and gem-hard eyes. "How is your pain?"

"My pain is fine."

My pain is on a lark. One to ten is meaningless. Give me something specific to go on. Why should I say *pain* when I can say *lancinating like a heated ice pick, scalding as a fumarole, penetrating as a fork tine in your tongue, clenching like a bowel loop?*

There's no pain scale for the pain of the pain your illness causes others.

"Tough titty, Miss Kitty. No pity party for you," my daughter said the morning of the Christmas craft fair. "Smoke dope," my therapist advised. "A little euphoria on the weekends won't hurt." After shopping at the mall we saw homeless people standing with their dogs at the bottom of the freeway ramp. I keep dollar bills and granola bars in the side pocket of the driver's door to hand out. "They're probably on drugs," my son's friend said from the back seat.

"I'd be on drugs, too," I said.

I get up to use the hospital bathroom. The floor in there is sticky with urine, and a pair of lacy underwear lies crumpled next to the commode. The ER hall of floating squares is lined with sticklike people, lumplike people, on gurneys wearing once-fancy coats—camel hair, boiled wool, lambs wool duffel—now stickered with leaves and grass. Regina once explained to me why homeless people emanate the stench of rot: it is untreated internal ulcers bleeding, it is the smell of blood digested. I make myself breathe in the bad smell and meet their eyes. I am part of the bad smell that meets the welcome wall of bleach when we are admitted upstairs, which after hours in the ER sparkles like a white-linoleum heaven.

They've given me oxycodone, and there are no pain numbers at all. Thoughts travel on dry darkness, trapezoids tumbling, spiders folded up in the desert, springing open. Walter reads a water-spotted *Sports Illustrated* in the frumpy recliner by my bed. This is not the stuff of lovers. I don't know how he stands to breathe in here. I swear I have shit out the inner lining of my intestines. I only eat breakfast. Lunch and dinner are slathered in gravy, brown gravy.

A nurse takes my blood pressure while wedging my forearm above her hip. This is the rhythm of my day—temp, blood pressure, IV bag, meal tray.

Sometimes when I say, "I love you," Walter doesn't say it back. It used to be I liked him for that, for the way it suspended my words, so I could hear how I meant them. I liked it because it let me know how wary he was of compulsion, compunction, obligation, all that can make these words an anchor against abandonment, like a night-light in every room. He prefers to find me in the dark.

From the hospital window I study the nineteenth-century building next door—stone cornices hold up urns of flowers, lion-headed sconces remind me how much I love Walter's lion-headedness between my legs. Beneath the sconces, ornate cabbage leaves birth stone ova.

"Walter," I whisper, reaching into the space between us.

"Unh hunh," he says, eyes not leaving the page.

The gastroenterologist, Dr. Volkov, makes an entrance, the curtain swishing behind her. She is round and comforting as a potato, but she moves with the full confidence of being middle-aged sexy. Her foundation color is slightly orange, her lips magenta, and she wears a purple-paisley scarf above her white lab coat.

"We do exam now, yes?"

I twist to roll over on my back, assuming she will want to poke and prod my abdomen.

"No, just the vey you are." She is snapping on yellow rubber gloves. It is quite an ensemble. Suddenly I understand.

"You vant him leave?" She nods toward Walter.

"No, he can stay."

Dr. Volkov grimaces and rolls her eyes. "However you vant."

Walter leans forward, takes my hands, smiles. "I always wanted to be part of a three-way," he says.

"Not like this," I say with a squeak as she slides a finger in and around.

"Ach," she says, as though we are impossible teenagers.

Later she will snap pictures of my glistening innards to a light box and speak without moving her jaw.

"Biopsy throughout colon. Intubated ileum. Proctitis present. Granulomas present. Defined location of disease. Slightly dilated bile ducts." Dr. Volkov pronounces her *s*'s with her tongue touching the roof of her mouth and her *o*'s like full moons. I love the elongated sounds. I stop hearing what she is saying, but Walter asks questions.

"Are these unusual symptoms?"

"All consistent vis ze disease."

"When will she be released?" he asks.

"Ah, yes," she says, "quvestion we all have, when will I be released?" She smiles at me, one gold incisor high and wolfish. "Three days, maybe?"

When she snaps off the light box and takes the films, Walter says, "I always wanted to get into your pants, but this is a little more than I expected."

I stare at him.

"That was supposed to be funny."

"I've got to call the children and my boss."

"Okay," he says. "And I could use a shower." He's gray in the face, pallid. The bags under his eyes have puffed out, and the lines around his mouth are haggard as dripping wax.

I call Guy, my ex. The phone has buttons and takes punches to the stomach well. Guy's silences are so long I mistake the holes in the receiver for a sieve and try to suck sound from him. It is very inconvenient that I am sick. He asks the same question Walter did: "When will you be released?" and he doesn't like the answer. So much silence is like siphoning gas; I never sense the contrapuntal moment to turn my head away, so in a fraction of a second I am gagging on vitriol.

"Guy, I'm in the hospital with a flare-up."

"It must be all those salads you eat."

"No, I think it's the disease."

"Okay, I'll tell the kids you're getting better, and you can make up the extra days when you get back."

I sink into the pillows. God forbid I should have one more child-free day in my life than he does, even if I spend it at the hospital.

A nurse with buzzed temples and a graying pompadour comes in to hang a new bag of antibiotics to the IV stand. In profile he looks like a dinged hatchet, like a country-western hero. "You happy as a clambake?" he asks. "My name is Winston."

"Oh, yeah," I answer. "Bring on the potato salad."

I notice that the fingernails on one of his hands are long.

"You play guitar?" I ask.

He smiles. "I pick some. Rockabilly mostly."

"Neat," I say.

"Let's see here," he says, reading off the chart while stroking his soul patch. "The patient does not tolerate Augmentin."

"That's right. I'm allergic to it. My forearm swelled to the size of a football."

He shakes the bag in front of his face. "Then why the hell did they give me a bag of Augmentin?"

"Please don't kill me," I say.

He looks directly at me. His eyes are jump-start blue. "I sincerely pledge not to." He unhooks the bag, muttering to himself. "Friday shift change . . . It's getting so no one can spell their own name around here." I half expect to hear shouting in the hall.

I take consolation in the 1969 version of *True Grit* playing on daytime TV. It's the scene where John Wayne as Rooster Cogburn charges Ned Pepper's gang on horseback.

"Now that was some riding," I say to Walter before I remember that he isn't in the room. I wonder briefly if he will he come back, or if I will be making remarks into empty rooms for some time to come. Then he texts me: "Much better now. Will bring u yr bathrobe."

How I hope my illness won't be a deal breaker . . . I hope, I hope, I hope, but I would rather take the rosy pill the nurse offers me. I call Noelle next, before the effects of the pill hit me.

"Mom, when are you coming home? Dad's so grumpy I don't even want to go out of the house with him."

"Try to cut him some slack," I say.

"He did buy me new workout clothes." She has already pivoted to his defense, then she pivots back to mine. "Mom, if you need to stay down there with Walter, that's okay. I want you to be well. I mean, I'll miss you and stuff."

"I'm not going to move away, Ellie, though Walter may move north when he retires. We're talking about it."

"That'd be cool," she says. "I like Walter. You'll get strong again, Mom."

"I know, honey. I've just got to listen—"

"—when the body talks," she says, completing my sentence, but she prefers to take the conversation elsewhere. "Remember that time we lost electricity for three days? You shoveled a ton of snow."

"I do remember. We put the meat from the freezer in the snow-bank."

"And you cross-country skied to the store for chocolate." She loves this version of me, as though reminding me of it will return me to it. "And we saw our neighbor riding down the hill on an upside-down ironing board."

"College students. What can you say?"

"If I needed to drop out of college, would you let me come home?"

"Of course, darling. But you're not even there yet."

"I know. I found a Christmas ornament from Grandma Rose behind Dad's couch."

"Is it cute?"

"Too cute. She's carrying a banner that says, 'Mothers are angels without wings.'"

"I like that."

"No way," said Noelle. "Mothers are devils without fangs."

I am placing the call to my son when Nurse Winston returns with a new IV bag, which he turns toward me before hanging it up. It reads, "Cipro." We nod at each other.

Norman tells me he has hacked his ex-girlfriend's Gmail account after reading her Facebook posts.

"Norman, get a hold of yourself. You and Julia are a bad combination."

The two of them have broken up three times already.

Norman says, "She's like a pancake, all golden brown and beautiful, until you flip it over and see it's all black and bubbly underneath."

"Norman—"

"If she posts on a military dating site, I'm going to post my bare ass for her profile pic." He laughs maniacally, then stops abruptly.

"It's funny, Mom—if I'm typing fast and leave out the r, I write girl-fiend instead of girlfriend."

I understand why he keeps going back to her. She has the high brow of an Italian angel and this lacy fringe of close hairs along her forehead and temples. She was raised Calvinist, but now she screams "Jesus loves you" out car windows when people flip her off. She was raised on a dairy farm until the family lost it, and she grew up pushing around Angus and Hereford cattle.

Last year I took Julia shopping at the secondhand-clothes store, before Christmas when the snow came. We found a pair of cute mukluks that laced up, and the laces were finished with little fur dingleberries.

"Will these be okay for all seasons?" she asked.

"No, honey," I said. "They're snow boots, and you need 'em." She had been wearing black canvas Keds from Kmart. It was twenty-two degrees out, and there were ice tongues across the pavement.

"Try not to hate her, son. She has done her best to love you despite all her troubles."

"Deep down, I know that, Mom, but anger is like slamming Jägermeister. I need to feel righteous to get through this. Anyway, how are you?"

"I've had a bit of a setback. I'm in the hospital with a Crohn's flare-up. It's under control."

"Well shit, Mom, why didn't you just bust out with it?"

"I'd rather hear your news."

"Is Walter there with you?" he sounds indignant, like he will come down here and punch Walter out if he doesn't treat me right.

For the time being, I think. "Yes, he's here," I say brightly. "He went back to his house to get my bathrobe and my book."

My son's sigh is audible. "Okay, well good. I can walk the dog when you get home, Mom, or he-man the groceries."

"Thanks, Norm. I may take you up on that."

"I love you, Mom."

"Even my black and bubbly underside?"

"Even your black and bubbly underside."

True Grit is over, and I can't imagine what is taking Walter so long. I find a large, angry bump on my shin. I start to cry. A rheumatologist came in yesterday and stroked both my shins, looking for vasculitis; now I've found it. I feel like a failed military strategist—I had the left flank covered, I had the right flank covered, but by God the enemy came across the river, the river I thought couldn't be crossed.

I feel myself take an emotional tumble. I have the physical sensation of plummeting. This vigilance is like walking on an incline in the fog, no depth of field at all; another sense comes into play, perception of mortal steep. I feel my skin prickle as my ears keen for the far-down sound of rushing water.

Winston comes in, and I cannot quell my blubbering. He perches on the side of my bed, hands clasped. He's wearing one of those rings made out of a bent fork and another with silver feathers bent around a chunk of turquoise.

"It could be an old spider bite," he says when I calm down.

"In a hospital?"

"Yeah, the bite doesn't look new. The rheumatologist probably already saw it."

I sob on anyway.

"Let's get you some Benadryl cream," he says, and I feel like a child in need of a Band-Aid to stop crying. "I can check with the rheumatologist."

He is turning to go when I blurt, "I'm afraid Walter is going to leave me now."

Winston doesn't blink. He doesn't even ask who Walter is. He returns to my bedside. "Now why would he do that?"

"Who would want me now?" I blub.

Winston sighs in an easygoing way. "Walter doesn't know what is going to happen to him next week. He could have a heart attack, and you could turn out to be the healthier one."

This goggles me sufficiently that I stop crying. "I don't want Walter to have a heart attack."

"Of course you don't. My point is people with chronic illness are actually healthier as they age."

"How's that?"

"Think about it. It's like a little old lady's car that is in such great shape because she drives it gently and takes good care of it."

I get this rush of well-being, the kind you have when you climb a mountain and your whole body pulsates. I feel I can ask Winston anything.

"How do you do this job? How do you handle it when people die?"

Winston looks out the window for a moment, musing. I wonder if he is contemplating the cabbage birthing ova in the scrolling architecture as I have.

He strokes his soul patch while speaking. "I don't think about death as death. I think about it as graduation, graduation from the planet." He shrugs. "But I've been depressed my whole life, so personally I'm looking forward to it."

I feel I need to think about this, and I feel weary without warning. I hear the metal rings of the curtain slide, and there is Walter—ruddy, burly Walter—a baguette in a brown wrapper rustling under his arm, a bouquet of plumeria emitting a blissful perfume, a mango bubble tea with a huge pink straw in his other hand. He looks from my damp face to the nurse and back again.

"We had a little scare, but we're over it now," Winston says, patting my leg as he rises. "I'll go get that Benadryl."

Walter breaks the crust of the baguette for me, and because we don't have a knife he presses whole pats of foiled butter onto each hunk. I eat as though each bite were a revelation, the smooth, cool fat of survival coating the roof of my mouth. I ask him to hold me, and he threads himself carefully through the IV tubes. I think I must have been a harbor seal in another life; I just want to lie humped against his bulk. The room fills with a cobalt cast, and the monitor next to the bed glows green as night falls. I can feel his belly warming my lower back.

"Walter?" I whisper.

"Mmmh."

"Are you going to leave me now?"

"Are you out of your mind?" He nuzzles the back of my neck. "Why would I do that?"

I don't touch the question; I pretend it's rhetorical. The balance of the moment is so perfect, so complete—a stone cairn standing on its own.

"In sickness and in health," he murmurs. "That's the deal, isn't it?"

"I'm not going to push myself anymore," I say, pushing myself into him.

"Oh, I highly doubt that," Walters says. "But maybe you won't push it so far."

"This can't be me," I whisper. "I'm a strong woman."

"You are," he says, "and when the doctor checks your knee for reflexes next month, you can kick a hole in his wall. But not today, darling. Not today."

I shut my eyes, willing this to be true.

Acknowledgments

With special thanks to my loving mother, for always encouraging my literary pursuits; to my children, Connor Cairns and Eveland Cairns, for choosing me and making me a better person; to my brothers, Andrew and Nathan, for living the puzzlement of our father alongside me; to Margi Fox, for being my big-hearted friend and peerless reader; to Priscilla Long, for encouraging me on the long road to publication; to Suzanne Paola, for candor about kids and keeping faith; to Suzanne Bair, for holding my feet to the ground and my toes to the fire with love; to Shawn Wong and Suzanne McConnell, for graciously giving me insight into the big picture; to Elise McHugh, in whose hands this book found its true shape; and to the Barbara Deming Memorial Fund, for recognizing this book when it wasn't yet a book.